"You can count
to give my life
That

Shane moved in front of Katherine, blocking her way. The music had stopped and all eyes were on the two of them.

"Great, now you've brought out the paparazzi, too. So much for hiding in plain sight," she said just as a camera's flash blinded her.

Shane trained his eyes on the person who'd taken that picture and that's when he saw it. There behind the roving photographer, a man dressed as a waiter stood silent, a gun trained on Katherine. In an instant, Shane pushed Katherine to the floor behind the table, threw himself down to shield her and screamed at the top of his lungs, "Everyone down. Now!"

A rush of panic hit the room. Shane held Katherine close, his heartbeat racing to match hers, his prayers asking for protection as he tried to get a line on the shooter.

In spite of the shouts, screams and confusion all around them, the man crouched and moved with purposeful intent, weaving between chairs and tables to finish the job.

And Katherine was the target.

LENORA WORTH

has written more than forty books, most of those for Steeple Hill. She has worked freelance for a local magazine, where she wrote monthly opinion columns, feature articles and social commentaries. She also wrote for the local paper for five years. Married to her high school sweetheart for thirty-five years, Lenora lives in Louisiana and has two grown children and a cat. She loves to read, take long walks, sit in her garden and go shoe shopping.

ASSIGNMENT: BODYGUARD

LENORA WORTH

Steeple Hill®

Published by Steeple Hill Books™

STEEPLE HILL BOOKS

Steeple
Hill®

Recycling programs
for this product may
not exist in your area.

ISBN-13: 978-0-373-44404-5

ASSIGNMENT: BODYGUARD

www.SteepleHill.com

Printed in U.S.A.

"But they lie in wait for their own blood;
they lurk secretly for their own lives. So are the
ways of everyone who is greedy for gain;
it takes away the life of its owners."
—*Proverbs* 1:18–19

To all of my Texas friends, with lots of love.

ONE

"Who is that handsome man wearing the tux?"

Katherine Barton Atkins thanked the waiter for her mineral water with a twist of lime, then glanced around at the woman who'd just asked that question. Red-haired Trudy Pearson had one elegant eyebrow raised in standard cougar mode while she stared across the crowded ballroom.

"Trudy, every man in the room has on a tux," Katherine explained, bemused and just a little morose because of Trudy's need to find a second husband, no matter what.

Some women just couldn't handle being alone, but Katherine was determined not to be one of those. She couldn't fault Trudy for trying, though. They were both widows now. Katherine had married her college sweetheart and Trudy had married an older man whom she'd loved with all her heart. And they'd both lost their husbands within six months of each other. After a year of being a widow, Katherine was trying to get on with her life while Trudy was trying to find a replacement. Katherine kept busy searching for something to fill her empty soul, while Trudy kept busy searching for a younger man because she was so afraid of growing old alone.

"Yes, darlin' Kit," Trudy replied in her sophisticated drawl, "every man in the room has on a tux, but only that man over there by the parlor fern knows how to *wear* one."

Curious, Katherine kept smiling at the people passing by her, then looked in the direction of Trudy's overly interested gaze, her expression shifting from disdain to dismissal as her gaze caught and held that of the man's. She took a sip of her cold water, the elegant bracelet watch Trudy had given her for her last birthday dangling down her arm. "Oh, *that* man wearing the tux. He's my detail."

"Excuse me," Trudy said, almost dropping her sparkling gold evening purse. "Your *detail?* What exactly does that mean? And I want *the details,* all of them. He's positively yummy. And that tuxedo is tailor-made for him and only him."

Kit touched her chignon then looked over at the tall, dark-haired man who was pretending he wasn't looking over at her. "My father thinks I need a bodyguard. I told you about those strange hang-up calls and then the cryptic letters I received. He's just being overly cautious because of this big crowd, I think."

Trudy glanced over at Katherine's father, Gerald Barton, who was standing with his wife, Sally Mae, talking to several other people. "Your daddy doesn't looked worried so why the detail?"

"Oh, he's not worried—*because* of the detail. You know my father hires only the best. And rumor has it this one is top of the line." She didn't want to give her friend the fact sheet on her bodyguard, nor did she tell Trudy about the feeling that someone had been in her house and office. She'd rather not talk about any of that tonight. She'd rather the bodyguard wasn't here in the first place.

But her father was a top-level member of CHAIM, the elite private security organization that worked to protect people the world over. That made him a bit tense and paranoid at times. He'd been worried about her since her husband Jacob had died, but when Katherine happened to mention a few unexplained calls and some of her files being moved and shuffled around, her father had gone into overdrive.

Katherine indulged her father because she knew he meant well, but sometimes his protective nature stifled her. Such as tonight.

"Top of the line is the word, darlin'," Trudy replied, her predatory gaze centered on the man. "He is the very definition of tall, dark and...dangerous."

Katherine couldn't help but laugh at her friend's description, but she tended to agree. At least this time, her father had hired a looker. "Yes, that's him, brought in all the way from London, England. He was hand-picked to look out for me tonight. But I'm trying to ignore him."

Trudy's burgundy silk gown rustled as she stepped closer. "British and in a tux. How on earth can you ignore *that,* do tell?" Then she gave Kit a wry smile that held just a trace of condescension. "Oh, let me guess. You can't say anything else about it, right?"

Her friend knew the complications of being the widow of a senator. And Trudy also knew that Katherine's father worked for a mysterious, secretive organization. But Trudy understood discretion and privacy. Besides, it was just too hard to explain right now.

"I'd rather *not* talk about it," Kit said, completely

aware that each time she moved an inch the dashing Sir Shane Warwick, known as the Knight, moved an inch with her. Turning away from the agent who worked for the covert Christian organization, she said, "This is a benefit, Trudy. I need to mingle with our patrons and thank them for their generosity toward the Barton Atkins Foundation." She put down the water she'd been nursing and whirled around, her cream-colored evening gown whispering around her legs, her matching high-heeled satin sandals making her feet scream for release. "Now why don't you quit ogling the man and help me greet my guests, okay?"

"Oh, all right," Trudy replied, turning to whisper something to a nearby waiter. Winking at the waiter, she pivoted back to Kit. "But later, you and I are going to have a serious talk. If you're in danger enough to need a handsome guard following you around, I need to know." Then she touched a hand to Kit's arm, her brown eyes turning serious. "I couldn't bear it if—"

"I'm fine," Kit said, wishing her father wasn't so overbearing. "It just goes with the territory."

Gerald Barton was one of the top agents in CHAIM— Christians for Amnesty, Intervention and Missions. And even though her father was supposedly retired, Kit had learned at an early age that a CHAIM agent never really retired. Especially when that agent's only daughter had lost her husband under questionable circumstances and was, herself, constantly receiving threats because of her stand against injustice.

Frustrated with the restrictions on her life, she shook her head then silently chastised herself. Maybe a prayer of thanks would be more appropriate, considering she was loved and held dear by her family and her friends.

And she was blessed beyond measure. Which made her quip, "I'd like to forget all of this, just for tonight, okay?"

Trudy nodded, then leaned in. "But, honey, you must be thinking the same thing I'm thinking. They never figured out what happened when Jacob's helicopter went down. That crash might not have been an accident, no matter how hard the authorities tried to do a cover-up."

"You don't have to remind me of that," Kit said, old hurts making her snap in spite of Trudy's concerns. "I think about it every day of my life." And she always hoped that somewhere in her philanthropic travels, she'd find out the truth regarding her husband's death. But no one was willing to delve into that now. It was over and done.

Lord, give me strength and patience, she silently prayed. *And teach me how to get over this deep grief.*

"I'm sorry," Trudy said. She dropped her arm and stood back. "Go do your job. But remember, you promised me you will take some time off for that spa trip we keep talking about. I've found a very secluded retreat out in New Mexico. Just the two of us. We need some downtime."

Kit looked at her watch again, thinking she'd need to make a speech in a few minutes. "That would be good. I've been so busy planning tonight's event, I think I'm a little overwrought. But, Trudy, thanks for your concern."

Trudy gave her a quick peck on the cheek, her worried look changing to playful as she touched a finger to Kit's pearls, lifting the strand for a second before she let the shimmering strand drop. "Whatever you think about him, that gorgeous man over there can't seem to take his eyes off you, darlin'."

"That's because he's being *paid* to keep his eyes *on* me," Katherine countered.

"And I'm sure he's enjoying his job," Trudy replied as she waltzed away and into the crowd. "Maybe you should enjoy the company."

Kit lifted her head, her hand going up to the single strand of pearls Jacob had given her for their tenth anniversary. They'd gone out to dinner and after they'd come home, he'd unclasped the pearls and hugged her close. They'd been fighting but he'd tried all that night to make up to her. "Promise me you'll wear these every single day."

"I promise," she'd said. That was the last time she'd held him in her arms. Her husband was dead now, and in many ways, so was she. At least she felt dead inside. Her devout mother and former CHAIM operative, Sally Mae, would tell her to never give up hope, to turn to her faith. But how could that help now?

What did it matter if she was receiving death threats for her determined stance? She had work to do and she intended to do it, and no amount of empty threats would stop her. Her work was the only thing holding Kit together these days. Work was her salvation. So with a renewed determination that included ignoring the handsome, dedicated man who'd been shadowing her all night, Katherine put on a convincing smile then moved through the glittering crowd filing into the hotel ballroom, her mind going on autopilot as she played to the hilt the role of hostess.

Head up, shoulders back, and a serene expression. That was the Barton tradition, after all.

* * *

He shouldn't have signed up for this. It was never a good idea to be in charge of taking care of a beautiful woman. Never a good idea, but then the Knight was known for taking on the tough cases. This one was killer tough. And so lovely.

Shane Warwick moved through the crowd, his gaze sweeping the room with a cool assessment. The ballroom was long and rectangular with shimmering crystal chandeliers and gleaming mirrored walls, which made it twice as hard to keep up with the subject under surveillance. Glass windows all around the big square room allowed an incredible view of downtown Austin, Texas, and the Colorado River, but Shane didn't have time to look out the windows. If he took his eyes off Katherine Barton Atkins long enough, he could enjoy the view of the State Capitol gleaming brightly off in the distance. But he couldn't look away from her and for more reasons than just this particular assignment required.

The woman was easy on the eyes, as they liked to say here in Texas.

Shane went over the facts, trying to distract himself from getting too involved. Getting involved with beautiful women was his gift and his downfall. Sometimes the job required certain things and sometimes he just fell hard for a pretty face then moved on once the excitement had worn off. He couldn't allow that to happen this time. Mainly because if Shane crossed that line with this woman, her father and his superior, Gerald Barton, would shoot first and ask questions later, as they also liked to say here in Texas.

Back to the facts, he sternly reminded himself.

Katherine "Kit" Barton Atkins, daughter of wealthy

CHAIM leader Gerald Barton and his wife, Sally Mae Barton, childless widow of State Senator Jacob Atkins, and CEO of the Barton Atkins Foundation. Old Texas money and all the perks and responsibilities of also inheriting her husband's newly minted money to boot.

According to the information he'd been given, the young widow wasn't a typical socialite. She believed in the causes she worked so hard for, even if it meant she had to attend such stuffy affairs as this one. And even if it meant she had to go out into the field and make her points with photo ops and highly opinionated, impassioned speeches. Plus, she didn't seem to mind getting down and dirty or going into the fray. He'd seen pictures of her holding dying infants in third world countries; he'd seen pictures of her walking through storm-littered villages. And he'd seen an unauthorized shot of her standing in a corner, turned slightly away from the glare of the spotlight, her hand to her face, all alone and wearing exquisite white pearls and a severe black dress, just after they'd buried her husband.

But she hid her grief behind her work and that was why he was here. Her father was very concerned about her. Which made Shane concerned, too, and intent on protecting her. If he could keep the woman in his line of sight.

She moved through the crowd with a grace that reminded Shane of ballerinas and swans and all things lovely. Her whole persona exuded cool, blond elegance. Her evening gown was almost severe in its cut and color—shimmering and sleeveless but with a discreet beaded beige portrait collar and a skirt that flowed all around her in soft, folding wisps of designer-cut silk. And she was wearing what looked like the same pearls she'd worn to her husband's funeral. Other than a pretty glittering watch on her left arm and her wedding band, the pearls were her only decoration. He wondered if she'd chosen this dress and jewelry on purpose—to set her apart from all the standard but predictable black and red formal dresses, festooned with sparkling jewels, fluttering all around her. Or had she just reached into her closet and come up with a winning combination of classic proportions? Either way, it worked for Shane.

Shane had always admired attractive women and he could spot a phony a mile away. Katherine was the real thing. Purebred and gracious, perfectly attired and perfectly serene. She seemed untouchable, unruffled and unconcerned, until she glanced up and straight into his eyes. Then she just looked determined and defiant.

Shane smiled to himself and put on his best game face. Kit was coming to greet him, at last. But she did not appear happy to see him.

"You're becoming a nuisance, Sir Warwick," she said as she walked up to him, a soft smile belying the dare in her pretty green eyes.

"Oh, really?" Shane took her hand and held it to his lips for the briefest of kisses. "And how's that, Mrs. Atkins, since you have yet to even acknowledge me. I was beginning to think I'd lost my touch."

She put a hand to her throat, diamonds twinkling on her finger. "Where are my manners?" Her smile didn't change, but the expression in her cat-like eyes certainly did. "I thought it wasn't proper for a woman to acknowledge the man her father hired to watch out for her, or was I wrong in that assumption?"

Shane adjusted his black tie. "Your father warned me

about your attitude. And that you'd spot me the minute I entered the room."

"Did he now?"

"He did indeed. Warned me about a lot of things. And told me not to let you out of my sight." He leaned close and gave her a smile that had reportedly melted feminine hearts all across the globe. "And I must say, I don't mind keeping my eyes on you at all. Your pictures don't do you justice. You are quite beautiful."

She inclined her head, pretending to enjoy being with him, even laughing for the benefit of those standing all around them. "Hmm. Let me see if I can get this straight. A dashing British secret agent in a precision-cut tux and a seemingly interested American woman in an overpriced evening gown. Their eyes meet across the crowded room, they walk toward each other, smiling and cordial…and the rest is written in the stars. Except I know how this ends. I've seen the movie. Your charms won't work on me, Sir Warwick."

Shane laughed out loud then looked into her eyes. She was actually very refreshing. Scary, but refreshing. "Ah, but you forgot the beautiful part."

She touched the pearls at her throat. "Excuse me?"

"The *beautiful* interested woman," he replied, smiling at his own cleverness. "And you *are* beautiful."

She smiled, too. That was a good sign, at least. Then she stopped smiling. "And you forgot the *seemingly* part, you know, as in the *seemingly* interested woman. Only this woman is not interested—so cut the charm, Warwick. I'm on to you and I don't like it one bit that you'd use charisma to try and win me over to allow you to hover around me. Get off my back, and give me some room here. I've got a full evening ahead of me and you're in the way."

Shane Warwick had to heave a surprised breath. There was a bit of fire underneath all that coolness, after all. "Your father also warned me that you'd try to lose me. But that, dear lady, isn't going to happen." There was only one way to handle such a bundle of bemusing contradictions and do his job at the same time, so he took her hand and whirled her out onto the dance floor. "I suggest we make the best of it...and dance."

He was rewarded with a gasp of surprise followed by a tight smile that told him only the most practiced rules of decorum were keeping her from slapping him across the face.

And because of that, Shane grinned down at her and reveled in the way she flowed right into his arms. This waltz might prove either to win her over, or do him in. He'd lay odds on the last scenario. He needed to do some serious praying for patience and control, and that God would allow him to do his duty and protect this woman.

So things would turn out differently this time.

Putting those dark thoughts out of his mind, Shane held her tight, and after taking some time to look into her brightly mad green eyes, he moved his gaze from her pretty face to the other faces in the crowd.

And he wondered the whole time if someone in this VIP crowd had been sent here to murder her.

TWO

Kit breathed in the fresh soapy smell of Shane's rich chocolate-colored hair. This wasn't fair, the way he held her in his arms with an aloof possession. This wasn't fair, the way her heart hurt from missing Jacob so much, the way her heart fluttered to life each time Shane bent his head and held her gaze with icy blue eyes, while he tried to search for all her secrets.

She wished her father hadn't hired this particular man, wished her husband was still alive to dance with her, and wished she could just run away to some quiet island and grieve, really grieve, for all she'd lost the day her husband had died. But a Barton had to be strong; a Barton showed no grief. And so she was expected to carry on. Duty called. And only manners kept her from doing exactly that—up and running out of this room. And away from this man.

"Am I making you uncomfortable?" he asked, his British accent precise and crisp in her ear.

"What do you think?" she shot back, looking up at him. "People are staring." Even her parents had stopped chatting to watch them move around the dance floor.

He dipped his head, his breath tickling against her

earlobe. "We could go somewhere more private so we can discuss my concerns for your safety."

"Nice try," she said, lifting away. "But I need to stay here with the people who paid a hefty sum to get in this room tonight, sorry."

He slid a glance around the room. "That's perfectly all right by me, Mrs. Atkins. Less danger in a crowd. But sooner or later, we will need to talk about your father's instructions."

Kit could agree with that, but not right now. "Sooner or later, we'll do that, maybe over a nice cup of tea," she said. "Just not tonight."

Apparently, he didn't like her response. "You are aware that you might be in danger, right?"

"Very aware." But the only danger she could see right now was the man dancing with her. No doubt, it was unwise to be alone with Shane Warwick. So she played her part and carried on until she could figure out what to do next.

"Call me Kit," she said, wondering why she'd decided to give him that liberty. "And I hate crowds, but I can't leave."

He smiled at that. "So you force yourself to do this, anyway? Because you believe in what you do even though events like this are sometimes tedious but necessary."

Surprised that he got her, she nodded. "Yes. I'm a rather shy, private person but I learned a long time ago I can't live that way. And I won't hide away like a coward, no matter what you and my father think. And no matter how big the crowd, and no matter the situation."

He studied her as they glided around the room. "I'm aware of the crowd, and very much aware of the situation. Heads are turning, whispers are surfacing, but that's not my concern right now."

"Well, it is mine," she replied. "People will talk."

"And you don't want them to, right? So what? The cool, elegant, tragic widow is dancing with a mysterious stranger. And right here in Austin, at that. Scandalous, but maybe exactly what you need right now. People need to think you have a new suitor."

Anger flashed through Kit. Did she seem that sad and pathetic? "I'm not that tragic, thank you. And I have to walk a thin line, to protect the organization I've worked so hard to build through the years, so you can't possibly know what I need."

The intimate look he gave her made her think he might know something about need himself, but right now, he didn't dare voice that—not out loud and to her face. His job was to convince her that she needed him for protection against something she couldn't even see in front of her. Something she didn't want to see. She only wanted to continue her work. And continuing this dance without guilt or worry of scandal might be nice, too, for a change.

He dropped the charm, almost startling her with the lightning fast way he'd changed. "Right now, I know that you need to take *this* situation very seriously. You're in danger and I'm here to keep you out of harm's way."

Kit's heart did a long shudder, fear tickling through her like a whispering warning for the first time tonight. "Why won't my father discuss this with me, so I can understand?"

"It's too complicated." He watched her for a minute, his icy eyes softening and never leaving her face. "There's been some chatter. Some of the threats you received were becoming very pointed and suggestive. And we've examined your home and office, based on files that have gone missing. It's enough to make Gerald think there's a need to be cautious. That's all you should know."

She lifted her chin. "I get that same line from my father. You know, I might be more willing and cooperative if someone would simply tell me what's going on. How can I be cautious if I don't know what I'm running from?"

"Good point." He looked at her with regret when the music ended. "Why don't we go sit down and I'll try to explain."

She checked her watch. "I have to give a thank-you speech in about fifteen minutes, Mr. Warwick."

"It's Shane," he replied, his smile back in let's pretend mode. "And not to worry on that account. I will be a perfect gentleman at all times and you can escape to give your speech without missing a beat. You have my word on that."

Kit believed him, and to her ultimate aggravation, was almost a little disappointed to cave so easily. Trudy was right about Shane Warwick. He knew how to wear a tuxedo. The man exuded cool, calm, collected and charming. Lethal qualities to tempt a woman who missed the closeness of marriage and a husband. But easing her loneliness wasn't why Shane Warwick was here.

Her powerful father had ordered him to watch over her. And Gerald Barton could pay for the best in everything, including bodyguards. She could rest easy in that assurance at least. Even if she probably wouldn't sleep a wink tonight when she finally made it home.

"We can take that table in the far corner by the orchestra," she told him, her gaze moving through the crowd. "We shouldn't be interrupted there."

"Good," Shane said, his approval telling her they'd also be safer there. "I'll get you settled and fetch us something to drink. Are you hungry?"

"No." She couldn't eat a bite if her life depended on it. Then she remembered why Shane was here. Her life might depend on following his orders, whether she wanted to or not. Dropping her defiance for now, she allowed him to guide her to their table.

The eyes of everyone in the room followed them with clear interest and curious speculation.

Shane set down their drinks and a plate of canapés then pulled out the chair across from her. The vase of red roses on the stark white brocade tablecloth added a sense of drama to their meeting. He'd taken on this job and now he had to do his best to convince the subject at hand that she needed to listen to reason. And, he decided on the spot, he hoped he could make her smile again in the process of getting acquainted with her.

Shane didn't know which part of his task would be the most difficult—keeping her safe or removing her mantle of grief. He hated the look of despair that came into her eyes when she didn't think anyone was watching. But he was paid to observe and paid to pick up on the slightest of nuances.

And right now, as he watched Kit from across the tiny table, he saw a woman who hid her emotions and her fears behind the aura of grace and style and proper grooming.

His mother, British-bred and born, would highly

approve of Katherine Atkins. But Lady Samantha wasn't here tonight, thankfully. He didn't need her playing matchmaker while he was on the clock. No, his dear mother was safely ensconced in their country home near London, entertaining a group of pretentious, titled friends who moved in royal circles. And having the time of her life doing it, he imagined.

"You're grinning," Kit said, her exquisite eyebrows lifting like a butterfly's wings. "Is this amusing to you?"

He shook his head. "I was thinking about my mother, actually."

Kit slanted her head. "That's not very complimentary of me, now is it? We're finally alone and you're thinking about your mother?"

He liked her sense of humor. "Trust me, luv, it was a passing thought. I was thinking how she'd love to meet you. She loves all things Texas, so much so that she married a Texan—my father was born and raised near Dallas. We still have property just outside Fort Worth." His smile tipped up into a grin. "And she named me after a movie—that Wyoming western *Shane*. I'm surprised she didn't name me Dallas, but my father loved that particular movie. Watched it all the time."

Kit leaned forward. "Well, I didn't know all of that. But you're so—"

"British?" he asked, following her body language and leaning forward a bit himself. "That I am. My mother's British with a lineage that dates back to Queen Elizabeth—the first Queen Elizabeth, that is." He shrugged. "My parents met on a cruise to Africa, went on safari together and well, as you said earlier, the rest was written in the stars. A true love match."

She lifted away, clearly uncomfortable with any talk of love matches. "Did your father move to England, then?"

"Yes and no. They lived there part of the time and here part of the time by mutual consent, and sometimes they even lived apart by mutual consent, but I attended school in England and spent most of my youth there, per my mother's request."

"And how did your father feel about that?"

"He brought me here during school breaks and the summers so we could hunt and fish and do manly things. Just so I'd have a well-rounded life, you understand."

"I do understand. Texas is so vast, we can all acquire a well-rounded life here. Even an Englishman."

His grin turned impish. "I think my mother would agree with you on that. She did spend a great deal of time in Texas when they were dating. Especially when he was trying to convince her to marry him. She said she almost backed out after meeting his loud, crude, slightly crazy family. But she grew to love them, one and all." He touched a rose petal and watched it fall to the table. "And she loved my father. Their time together wasn't always happy, though. I think they needed their spots of separation."

She frowned. "I thought you said it was a love match."

"I did and it was. But all good things take time and compromise, or as my mother calls it—mutual consent and mutual respect." He looked at her, her eyes, her lips, her long, elegant throat, that enticing strand of perfect pearls. "But some things can be worth the wait."

Kit, following the line of his gaze, toyed with her

pearls. "So she didn't give in at first, even though she was in love with him?"

Shane saw the interest in her pretty green eyes. And a bit of sadness. She was a romantic then. "No, he used to say he chased her until she let him catch her. And she used to say that she had him wrapped around her finger, but she just wanted to make sure he sweated a little before she said yes."

"What a charming story."

Shane nodded, took a sip of his drink. "My father, William, died a few years ago. So now, it's hard for Lady Samantha to come to Texas. It reminds her too much of him."

Kit put her elbow on the table then dropped her chin onto her upturned hand, making her look more like a fresh-faced debutante than an attractive, mature woman. "I can certainly understand that feeling. Sometimes, I'd like to get out of this state myself."

Shane noted that. "I'm sorry for your loss. From what I've heard, your husband was a good man."

She blinked, realized she wasn't sitting up properly and just like that, her spine went ramrod straight, no longer touching the back of her chair, while the curtain on her emotions came down with a feminine sigh and an elegant lifting of her chin. "Thank you. Now let's talk about why you're here and what I need to do to make this as unobtrusive as possible."

Shane put his hand on his heart. "Unobtrusive? You want *me* to be unobtrusive?" She didn't need to know that he was an expert at sneaking in and out of most places completely undetected.

She actually laughed and the sound of it flowed over Shane's highly aware nerve endings like delicate bells moving through a warm wind. "What? You've never tried being that way before?"

"Not in my arsenal, I'm afraid. I prefer to operate on the principle of hiding in plain sight. I like to be out there, very visible, but very aware. My plan is to be seen with you a lot, so that the society ladies who love to gossip over lunch at the club or while hitting tennis balls back and forth on the court, will take notice and spread the word. I want us to be seen as an item."

"Your premise being?"

"My premise being that an attached woman is much safer than a single, alone woman." He shrugged. "And besides, it will make my job that much easier."

Her eyes went dark again. "I am single and alone and I've learned to live with that, regardless of making your life easier."

Shane hated himself for making her think along those lines but it was necessary for her safety. "All the more reason to seem involved. My presence could throw off a potential enemy."

"Or invite that enemy to fight to the finish."

"I see you know more about your father's work than you let on."

"Yes, more than I want to know." She pushed at her immaculate upswept white-blond hair. "I don't like living this way. I don't want to walk around in fear."

"You won't have to if I'm with you."

"But how long will this ploy work? Are you prepared to stay by my side all the time, even when I leave the country?"

His pulse quickened at that. "Especially if you leave the country—make that—if you're *allowed* to leave the country. I have my orders."

"Of course you do. And I like my privacy and my dignity, and I won't be told what I can and can't do. So I don't intend to be part of some facade or deception. It's not right."

"It is right if it means saving your life, Katherine."

She stood up, dismissing him in a shimmer of silk and a whiff of lily-scented perfume. "That's the CHAIM way, isn't it? Always. Might makes right. All for the good fight, the good cause. Do you ever get tired of all the secrecy and the conspiracy?"

Shane almost answered yes to that question. Yes, he did get tired, of war, of the horrors of injustice, of all that he'd seen in his covert travels around the planet, but he'd joined this organization after his father had introduced him to Gerald Barton. They'd both seen something in Shane that he hadn't even seen in himself. A restless need to avenge good people, to help save lives when innocence clashed with evil, when good men had to fight ruthless criminals that no amount of man's law could stop. He'd been trained from birth to hunt, shoot, and fight like a gentleman—at his mother's insistence, but with his father's help, he'd learn how to think like a combination street gang fighter and gunslinger, with purposeful intent and take-no-prisoners determination. And even though he might sometimes have to get down and dirty to do his job, he worked to fight the good fight and he believed in saving lives, not taking them. So he looked up at Katherine Atkins and said nothing.

"Your silence speaks volumes," she said, whirling to leave.

Shane was up and by her side in a flash. "There are some things a lady doesn't need to hear."

She glared up at him, her eyes a sea of unfathomable

green. "And there are some things a gentleman should tell a lady. Such as what kind of danger she is in and why? But your loyalty lies with my father and CHAIM, right? So I can't count on you to tell me the truth."

He moved in front of her, blocking her way while those curious gazes all around the room stayed centered on them. They'd make the society columns tomorrow and that would work just fine with their cover. "You can count on me to protect you, to give my life for you if necessary. That is my job."

"Don't you think you're being a bit overly dramatic?"

"Don't you think you could possibly avoid making a scene and listen to reason?"

She looked around, realizing much too late that the room had grown quiet, that the orchestra was on a break. The music had stopped and all eyes were on the two of them.

"This is your fault," she said just as a camera's flash blinded her. "Great, now you've brought out the paparazzi, too. So much for hiding in plain sight."

Shane trained his eyes on the person who'd taken that picture and that's when he saw it. Just a flash in the crowd, a quick bit of action that seemed entirely out of place. There behind the roving photographer, a man dressed as a waiter stood silent and still near an exit on the other side of the orchestra stage, not far from where they were. Shane directed his gaze to the man holding the linen napkin across one arm and saw in that one second, as his gaze locked with the other man's, that the man had a gun trained on Katherine.

In a move that he'd remember later as pure adrenaline, Shane pushed Katherine to the floor behind the table, threw himself down to shield her and screamed at the top of his lungs, "Everyone down. Now!"

A rush of panic hit the room and then bullets started flying all around them. Chaos took over as people either ducked or ran for the nearest exit. But there in the corner behind the protection of a flimsy table, Shane held Katherine's trembling body close to his, his heartbeat racing to match hers, his prayers asking for protection as he tried to get a line on the shooter crouching near the big stage.

Speaking with shouted emphasis into his earpiece, he called for backup, his gaze never leaving the determined shooter. In spite of the shouts, screams and confusion all around them, the man crouched and moved with purposeful intent, weaving between chairs and tables to finish the job.

And Katherine was the target.

"Don't move," he whispered into Katherine's ear. "We're going to get you out of here, just hold on."

Then he reached for the Glock semi-automatic pistol he was carrying in a shoulder holster underneath his tuxedo.

THREE

She couldn't breathe.

Kit twisted, her hands clutching one of the lapels of Shane's tuxedo. He'd shielded her, putting his body between her and the bullets, and now he was trying to peek around the table. He had a sleek, strange-looking gun in his hand. This was real, too real.

"Shane?"

He didn't answer at first. His body tensed, his gaze fixed on someone across the room.

"I'm here," he finally said, giving her a quick look. "Stay down. I'm right here. But Katherine, listen to me, all right?"

"I'm listening," she said, wanting to laugh. He'd tried all night to make her listen but now that she was tossed in a corner like a sack of potatoes—her dress torn, her hair coming undone, and someone hiding in the now-silent room with a gun—she was willing to listen. More than willing. She listened just to hear Shane's breath.

"Kit, could you let go of my jacket?"

Mortified that she was holding on to Shane for dear life, she dropped her white-knuckled hand. "I'm sorry."

"No need to apologize. I want to get a better angle. And I want you to stay behind this table, understand?"

She lifted her head then took her first real breath since he'd pushed her down behind the table. And with that breath, she was back in action herself, her fear turning to a rage that screamed for release. "Shane, I can't stay down here while others are in danger. There are a lot of people in this room besides me. Let me up."

"No, no. I mean it, Kit. You can't—"

"How many?" she asked in a tight whisper.

Shane pushed her back down. "Not now. Stay down."

"How many shooters?" she asked again, her hand now gripping his arm.

He actually appeared shocked. He blinked, looked back at her. "Only one, so far. And if you'll let go of my arm, he won't be around much longer."

"Are you going to kill him right here?"

He watched the still room for movement. "Would you prefer I take him out back and throw him to the hogs?"

"There are no hogs in downtown Austin," she replied, her words growing stronger. "But I know where a mean, old bull lives."

He shot her a worried smile. "You're in shock. It'll pass."

"I am not in shock. I'm mad," she said on a hiss of breath. "And I've got a cramp in my foot."

"Well, I wish that's all you had to worry about, Katherine. Now let go of me and stay down and we'll talk about the mean bull later."

She finally released his arm. "What's the plan?"

"I'm not quite sure," he whispered back. "I'm making it up as I go."

"Some bodyguard you are."

"Yes, right on that." He flipped the table onto its side so fast she didn't even see it fall. A few people down around them gasped but Shane held up a hand to silence them. "Get behind this and stay here. Do not move." And then, in a flash of black, he was rolling away from her and gone.

"Shane?"

He didn't answer. She heard people whispering in fear all around her then glanced up for the first time to find Trudy huddled with a man behind the buffet table—the head of catering of all people. Motioning, Kit held up a thumb toward her friend.

Trudy returned the thumbs-up and shot her a wan smile. Then Kit heard a loud thud, followed by a deep groan. She closed her eyes, praying that Shane wasn't dead. She willed him not to die, not tonight while he was trying to save her. She couldn't bear that kind of guilt, especially after she'd tried so hard to ignore him and discourage him. But Shane was a good man. She could see that now. He had such a nice smile and he had this air of self-assurance that she'd never witnessed in another man. Not even Jacob.

"Jacob," she whispered, her heart breaking with longing, her head down and her hand over her mouth. "Jacob, I need you here. Why did you go away?" She didn't voice her prayer, but heard it clearly in her head. *Dear Lord, I need You to help all of us. Don't let anyone die tonight.*

She saw a masculine hand set against a crisp white

cuff reaching toward her. The cuff link winked bright and bold and looked like some sort of ancient coat-of-arms. Katherine blinked, thinking this must all be a dream. But the hand reached down toward her with an impatient shake so she had no choice but to take hold of it. She reached up and felt the man's fingers wrapping around hers, a stirring warmth penetrating the numbness that had frozen her entire system. She gazed up and into Shane's crystal blue eyes.

"Come with me," he said, his tone curt and no-nonsense.

Katherine got up but stumbled, her knees refusing to hold her. Then she was swept clear of the floor and into his arms. Wrapping her hands around his neck, she turned away from the few people still hiding in the room and trained her eyes on him. Only him. She heard Shane barking orders, heard her father speaking loudly to the hotel security.

Shane's voice carried through the ballroom. "One shooter, secured. He went down on the right side of the stage, still alive. I'll give a full statement later. I'm getting her out of here."

The room sounded with cries and feet rustling and people running across the marble floor. They were all asking rapid-fire questions, men angry and women crying. The music would not start back up now, of course. It had been put silent by a killer's intent.

Katherine heard all of it through the muffled protection of Shane's rock-solid shoulder bearing the weight of her head, but she couldn't face the people and the questions and…she didn't dare ask what had happened to the other man.

* * *

"He's still unconscious. But I reckon he won't talk when he does wake up."

Shane looked from Gerald Barton to the two other men sitting in the darkly paneled study. They were back at the CHAIM fortress called Eagle Rock, in the secluded hill country just on the outskirts of Austin.

"He will soon enough," Alfred Anderson said. "The Austin police will see to that."

John Simpson grunted then took a long swig of coffee. "But he might rather be charged, tried and put away for a long time. Because if he speaks, he knows he could die inside prison or out. Smells like a deliberate hit to me."

Gerald got up to stomp around the massive conference room. "At least she's safe here." Then he glanced at Shane. "She is safe here, isn't she, Warwick?"

Shane used to be sure about such things, but tonight, he wasn't so sure. He'd given a detailed statement to the locals and he'd gone over everything with his CHAIM supervisors. But something didn't seem right. His ulcer was shouting a warning with quick spasms of heat. Pulling out a roll of antacid tablets, he chewed one then said, "I have some concerns, sir."

Gerald looked affronted. "C'mon, Knight, you helped rebuild the security system in this place. Kissie and you both said no one can get in here."

"What if someone is *already* in here?" Shane said. "It's happened before."

Gerald nodded. "He's right. Devon Malone almost lost Lydia Cantrell because one of the servants wasn't just here to fold napkins and plan meals. Tried to smother the poor girl with a pillow."

"We've tightened things since then," Alfred said. "My wife made sure of that. She was not happy that we'd let an assassin serve us dinner, let me tell you."

In spite of the image of tiny, spry Lulu Anderson being peeved about a renegade butler, Shane still had his doubts. Something about this whole night didn't make sense.

They'd made sure the hotel ballroom was secure, which meant someone on the inside had set this up. That was the only clear explanation. Or maybe he wasn't *thinking* very clearly since he couldn't stop thinking about Katherine Atkins. Think about the assignment, not the client, he reminded himself. He should have learned from past experiences to stay focused.

And yet, he couldn't get the image out of his mind of Katherine's hand reaching up to take his. Or the feel of her soft skin brushing against his.

"I just want to be sure we're doing the right thing, sir. Another location might be more advisable at this point since we could have been followed. We need to get her away from Austin."

Eagle Rock was Fort Knox—impenetrable and tightly secure, with everything from fingerprint and facial scanners to keypads with state-of-the-art biometric security. Which is why Shane had brought Katherine straight here, rather than take her to her home in Austin. This sprawling ranch-style mansion held eight bedrooms and as many adjoining baths, an industrial size kitchen and a long dining room, a huge den and several smaller offices, not to mention several outbuildings and a private airstrip. Each of those areas could be sealed off from the rest with a flip of a switch. Not exactly a great way to live, but necessary in their line of work.

And usually, CHAIM agents only came here for conferences and training sessions, or to be interrogated when an operation had gone wrong. Which it almost had tonight.

"I didn't do my job tonight," he said, whirling to stare at the three men who, although retired, were still listed as his immediate superiors in a crisis such as this. "I should have been more vigilant."

"Warwick, we've gone over this," Gerald said. "I was there in the room, too, son, and I never saw this coming." His shrug said it all. "We checked everyone who entered that place, especially the hired help. I can't figure how that man got past security with that gun."

"That's just it," Shane said, logic coloring his words. "He didn't. Someone had to give him the gun or put it where he could find it. Someone from the inside."

"Well, thankfully we got the man alive. And you saved my daughter's life," Gerald replied.

"But I was assigned to watch her," Shane said, looking down at his discarded, black bow tie, his mind whirling with images of people running and screaming and a lone gunman standing near an exit door, his sleek gun held with one hand just underneath the shield of his other raised arm. And aimed right toward Katherine Atkins.

"If that camera flash hadn't gone off, she would have died right there beside me."

"But that's the fact, Warwick," John said. "You *were* right there beside her and your quick actions saved her. And a lot more people, too."

Gerald nodded, his fingers thumping on the table. "And that fancy stun gun you carry around put the shooter out cold. Fancy little gadget, that thing. Left a bullet hole in that man's shoulder but kept him alive for questioning."

Well, a Glock .357 with a suppressor wasn't exactly a stun gun, but this was Texas after all. These men were better suited to rifles and shotguns, or maybe six-shooters.

Shane went back over the details. "It was chaos at first, but a lot of the guests did manage to get out of the room. The few who were left stayed behind tables and doors. Thank goodness we only had two wounded and no one dead."

Yet he couldn't get the memories of shattering glass and frightened screams out of his mind. Nor the image of Kit reaching up a hand to take his after he'd felled the crouching shooter, her eyes locking with his when he'd lifted her into his arms and carried her out of the room. He could still smell the scent of lilies on his clothes.

And he still had to wonder if the shooter, who'd also had a silencer on his gun, had been there alone. Or if this had been carefully planned by someone close to Katherine.

"The papers will be all over this tomorrow morning," John warned. "But it can't be helped. The official word will be that someone allegedly came into the room with a gun, but was apprehended and arrested on the scene. It'll be listed as an attempted robbery due to the elite crowd, most of them wearing expensive baubles and carrying big wallets. We don't want any more information than necessary leaking out, especially anything regarding Katherine being the target."

"As far as I know, none of the people there are aware of that," Shane said, not ready to voice what his instincts seemed to be shouting. "And frankly, gentlemen, I didn't stick around to do damage control. My only intent once the shooter was secured was to get Katherine to a safe location."

John Simpson glanced over at Gerald. "And we've put out the word that Katherine and you have been dating, so you've taken her to a secluded location to get over the shock of what happened. That way, the press can leave her alone. We hope. The official statement should be in the papers and on the news tomorrow."

"That's our best cover," Shane agreed. And that's exactly what he'd planned to insinuate to the public— that they were an item. Well, the best laid plans of mice and men...

"You did the right thing, bringing her here," Gerald said. "You have my gratitude."

"I'd like to check on her," Shane said, wondering if he'd be dismissed or watched himself. These three men were some of the original five-man team that had started CHAIM all those years ago, halfway around the globe while they'd all served their country in Vietnam and later, other areas of the world. They were still a force to be reckoned with. "If I may have your permission, Gerald."

Gerald gave him a mean-hard stare, but nodded. "Her mama's in there with her right now. And trust me, son, you don't want Sally Mae getting her dander up again tonight. She was in a real tear about her daughter almost getting shot, let me tell you. I should have sicced her on that gunman. She'd get some answers."

"I do believe she would have, sir."

Gerald ran a hand over his silver hair. "Better give them some time together before you go knocking on any doors."

"Duly noted," Shane said, his smile tired. Sally Mae had nearly taken down the house earlier, demanding to see her daughter, and she didn't care if it hair-lipped the governor. Frightful woman she was when she was in a tizzy. "I'll be out on the back patio then."

He took his leave, knowing they'd want to discuss this latest development in private. He'd get his orders soon enough. But right now, he needed some time to digest all that had taken place. And he needed to find a way to make sure an incident such as this never happened again. Because that shooter had been a hired expert. Hired from someone high up and able to afford an assassin. Shane couldn't get the notion out of his head that maybe that same someone had been in the crowd tonight.

He had to get Kit to safety. And that meant away from Austin and away from Eagle Rock. He knew how to hide a person. And besides, he knew exactly which room they'd whisked Kit off to earlier and he wasn't above breaking into that room to make sure she was safe.

She might not ever feel safe again. In spite of having a warm bath and putting on a soft cotton tunic, matching pants and a cashmere robe someone had handed her a few minutes ago, Kit felt cold and clammy. But she held herself tightly together because she refused to shiver in fear.

"Honey, why don't you lie down?"

Kit turned from the drape-covered, bulletproof window to find her mother hovering near the brocade sofa of the cozy sitting room just off the bedroom. "I'm not sleepy, Mother."

"I could give you something," Sally Mae Barton said, reaching into her purse. "I have a sedative."

"I'm not taking a pill either," Kit said. "I just want to go to my own home. When can I leave Eagle Rock?"

"Oh, now, honey, I don't know about that. Your daddy is in a real pickle about what happened. I can't say when you'll be able to leave."

"You can't be serious," Kit said, pacing in front of the fireplace. It was late summer and humid even at this hour, but she thought about building a fire. Only, someone would rush to stop her. Too many people were hovering around her tonight, stifling her with well-meaning concern. She just wanted to get away from it all.

She thought of Shane and wondered where he was. Had they sent him away? No, her father wouldn't do that. He liked Shane and trusted him or he wouldn't have brought him here. Shane had done everything in his power to help her, and she owed him her life. He'd saved a lot of people's lives tonight.

"I want to see Shane," she announced to her mother.

Sally Mae lifted a slender hand through her dark hair. "I don't think that's wise, darlin'. It's late and he's in with the others right now. You just need to rest."

Kit wasn't about to rest. "Mother, I can't sleep. I'm too keyed up. And I'd like to talk to the man who put his life on the line in order to save mine tonight."

Sally Mae stood to her five-feet-two-inch height. "You can't do that, Katherine."

Katherine wasn't having any of that. Her mother might have been a CHAIM operative in her heyday, but she wasn't going to bully Kit with that superior attitude. "Mother, I want to see Shane and if I have to scream at the top of my lungs and sound every alarm in this stucco and brick fortress, I'll do it. I've had about enough for one night."

"I'll go see if I can find him," Sally Mae said, her tone even-keeled. "But only if you promise to rest after you see him."

Kit nodded, waving a hand. "That's a deal."

Sally Mae looked doubtful. "Do you want me to get Lulu or Rita in here to sit with you? They're both in their rooms but I have them on standby."

"No, I'm fine," Katherine replied, thinking her mother's friends would put her in a chair and give her a facial to soothe her frayed nerves. She didn't want a facial. She wanted to see Shane. "Honestly, Mother, I'll be fine."

She watched as her mother hurried out of the room still wearing her teal blue ball gown and matching kitten-heeled pumps. Kit loved her mother, but Sally Mae was just as protective as her father. They only cared about her welfare, she knew. And she appreciated and respected both of them.

"But right now, I just need—"

"You rang?" a voice called from the bathroom.

"Shane?" She rushed across the soft carpet and into the wide, open bath, her heart doing a strange little dance. "How'd you—"

"Trade secret," he said, pointing to the wide, square window over the garden tub. "I broke in."

"But the alarms didn't go off."

"Of course not," he said, adjusting his jacket. "I helped develop the security system in this place last time they updated it. Even Kissie herself said I did a good job." He checked the window. "I simply went to the main frame and reset the timers back long enough to allow me to enter the building in an unconventional way." He looked at his gold watch. "They'll reset in about…three seconds."

Kit heard a soft beep, beep coming from the monitor on the wall. "And what if my father notices?"

"He won't. I only did it for this wing of the house. And I knew the exact time when the live feed to the security room switches cameras. Plus, your mother won't allow any visual monitors in your bath. That would be an invasion of privacy."

He stopped talking and looked at her, his tone going soft as his crystal-shot gaze swept over her. "I had to see you." He lifted a finger toward her face to push a strand of hair off her cheek. "I like your hair down."

Kit lowered her head, suddenly feeling the need to burst into tears. But she held herself in check, figuring all of these strange, electric emotions were due to the scare of almost being shot. She wouldn't fall apart, not tonight. And not in front of him. "I'm okay. I just sent Mother to find you."

"I heard you from my spot in the shrubbery. And I'm here."

Before she could say anything, he took her hands in his. "Are you all right?"

She nodded, the warmth and strength of his fingers bringing the life back to her limbs. She allowed her gaze to wander away from his eyes for just a minute. He'd lost the bowtie and now his shirt was opened at the throat. Even rumpled and fatigued, he was still a striking man. Katherine decided she'd better focus on his face. But that didn't help matters. His expression held an edge of anticipation capped off with weariness. And guilt.

"I'm okay, really, I am," she said. "Is my friend Trudy Pearson okay? They wouldn't let me check on her."

"I saw her, yes. She was a bit shaken but she's fine. She went home, but only after I promised her you were safe. I'm pretty sure her new friend—the hotel employee she befriended while under fire—was going to escort her to be sure."

Katherine smiled at that. Leave it to Trudy to find a date even in the face of attempted murder. "Good. I'm glad."

"Katherine, why did you want to see me? Did you remember something or see something tonight that I need to know?"

She stared up at him, seeing the solid concern in his eyes. "Oh, no. I mean, I can't remember anything that would help. I…I just wanted to thank you, for saving my life."

He leaned close, his eyes flaring as his gaze held hers, the sincerity in his words endearing him to her. "It was my duty and my honor."

"It's not over yet, is it?"

"No, I'm afraid not."

"Where do we go from here?" she asked, gripping his hands to ward off the trembles moving through her body.

"I'm working on that. The shooter is in the hospital and under police custody but he's still unconscious. Our people and the police have gotten statements from all the eyewitnesses, but no one has come forward yet with any solid explanations or motives." He leaned close then, his words a whisper in her ear. "And I'm not so sure you're safe, even here."

Shocked, she pulled back. "You can't be serious."

His touch moved up her arms, protective and intimate. "I think you're still in danger."

"But this is Eagle Rock. I've always felt safe here."

"Things have changed," he retorted, his eyes locking with hers, one hand going to his stomach as if he were in pain. "I've got a bad feeling."

"So what do you suggest?"

"I have a plan, if you're willing to trust me." Holding her shoulders again, he leaned forward and asked, "How would you like to run away with me?"

FOUR

Katherine opened her mouth but her words only came out in a whisper. "What do you mean?"

"As I said, I'm not so sure you're safe in Austin, even here at Eagle Rock. Devon's wife Lydia was attacked here a couple of years ago, before they were married. They were on the run and came here to hide."

"I remember. Mother told me their story. Devon had a target on his back and Lydia got caught in the crossfire. And it involved Eli Trudeau's grandfather Pierre Savoy."

"Yes, because his grandfather—the Peacemaker and one of the founding members of CHAIM—wanted them both dead so he planted someone on the inside to do the job, or at least to kill Lydia."

"You don't think—?"

"I'm not paid to just think. I'm paid to act. Someone smuggled a weapon into that room tonight in spite of our best security measures. It had to be someone above suspicion but with easy access to the event. And that means the same person could also reach you here. So as I said, I have a plan but your father and his cronies won't like it. Are you interested?"

Katherine looked around at the place where she'd

always come for extended visits growing up. While the Andersons lived here year round and took care of the compound, Eagle Rock was like her second home. She'd spent so much time here and never once had she questioned her safety.

Until now.

Should she trust the CHAIM system or the man who'd broken into this room to make sure she was all right? The same man who'd saved her life tonight?

"How can I be sure of anything?" she asked.

"You can't. Nor can I. I usually rely on my experience and my training, my instincts and…a lot of prayer."

"I've been praying since this happened. I'm hoping God will give me understanding until we can find out why this is happening to me."

"That's my job," he said, "if you're willing to trust me and let me do that job."

She looked up at Shane, her hands trembling again. He took her hand in his, waiting for her answer.

"What did you have in mind?" she finally asked.

He leaned down to whisper in her ear. "Well, first, we have to break out of Eagle Rock. And after that, well, we'll be on our own until I can do some digging and put all the pieces together. But Kit, I can't do this if you don't feel…if you aren't sure."

She didn't know if it was because she was in shock or just tired of fighting, but she shook her head, her blood pulsing back to life. "I'm not sure."

He looked disappointed, but he nodded understanding. "Then we'll go to plan B."

"And what is that?"

He gave her a soft grin. "I'll just have to take you hostage."

"You're not serious."

"No. But it's tempting."

"But won't we be in even more danger out there?"

"Not where I'm going," he said. He rubbed his stomach. "I can't shake this feeling."

She faced him, her world tumbling and crashing much too fast. She wasn't used to this. She liked stability and structure and calendars and committees. Those things kept her on track and helped her to focus on helping others. But how could she be a good steward if she was putting everyone in danger?

The room was still and hushed, but Shane didn't push her. The silence didn't seem to faze him. She supposed he was used to silence.

Finally, she swallowed, pushing away the solid wall of fear. "I didn't say I wouldn't do it. I don't think I have any choice. I didn't take these threats seriously before, but if that man was after me then my presence at that gala put others in danger. Maybe it would be best if you and I did leave."

He lowered his head. "Is that a yes?"

Her prayers lifted with each heartbeat. "Yes."

He gave her a quick peck on the cheek. "Okay, we're going to have to act very quickly and I need you to do exactly as I say. Are you up to it?"

"I want my life back," she said. "And Shane, I think my father hired the right man to make that happen, regardless of *how* you make it happen."

He took her hand in his and kissed it, then bowed deep. "At your service, Madame. Now let's get you into some decent traveling clothes. And pack a bag. We'll be gone for a while."

Katherine hurried to change, her mind whirling with

a renewed awareness. Her trembling had shifted to nervous energy, but she couldn't decide if she was running away from danger or using that as an excuse to run right into Shane Warwick's waiting arms.

Kit's mind raced with worry and anticipation, her prayers scattered. Worry that she was making a drastic mistake and anticipation that she would finally be free of the yoke of propriety that had held her since she was presented as Cotillion Queen back during her college years.

"How are you coming in there?" Shane asked from the sitting room, his pacing making her even more nervous.

Kit put on her watch and her pearls—silly but necessary for her sanity. "I'm almost ready."

Was she? Kit knew how to pack a light travel bag. She usually kept things packed and ready to go at home, since she sometimes had to travel at a moment's notice. But here at Eagle Rock, things were different. Her mother and Lulu Anderson kept clothes here in various sizes for all the wives of the CHAIM agents—maybe because Sally Mae instinctively knew her friends might have to leave quickly? But Kit was so confused, she could only stare at the huge walk-in closet full of feminine things. What to take?

Black, she decided. A lady could never go wrong with black, even when she was on the run from someone who obviously wanted her dead. Trying to keep her head with a little bit of humor, she grabbed a slinky black travel set—pants and a matching lightweight duster. That would work on the run, wouldn't it? After adding a few other things, she grabbed an overnight bag from a shelf then stood still, the enormity of her situation making her numb.

She whirled to find Shane staring at her from the doorway. "Don't analyze your wardrobe, Katherine. We have no time for that."

She lifted her chin. "What do you suggest then for someone who's got a target on her back?"

With a grunt and just a bit of sympathy in his eyes, he gently pushed her aside and started grabbing at garments. "Jeans—they're sturdy and fit in anywhere. Some T-shirts and jackets and good walking shoes."

She watched as he selected various items and tossed them in the open bag she'd found in the closet. But he held her cell phone out then dropped it in his pocket. "There. You'll make a statement, I'm sure. And you'll live to buy more clothes."

"Can you guarantee that?" she asked, smarting from his obvious impatience and his misunderstanding of her hesitation. "Can you promise me that my presence won't get someone else killed?"

He zipped the bag. "I can assure you that while you're in my care, *you* won't get killed."

While you're in my care.

His words, spoken in a low, gravelly voice, flowed through her like a gentle rain. Not "While I'm trying to protect you." Not "While I'm trying to keep you alive." But "While you're in my care." And not a promise, but an assurance. Was there a difference?

The man had a way of saying things.

"I'm ready," she said, sending up one last prayer for hope and guidance.

They made it to the door just before it burst open.

Sally Mae Barton saw the overnight bag, and shook

her head. "Oh, no. You are not taking my daughter out of here."

"Mother—"

Sally Mae pointed at Kit. "You can't leave. Your daddy will blow his top. He wants you here where he can keep an eye on you."

Shane stepped forward, his stance at once protective and formidable. "I want to get her out of here because I don't believe she's safe here, Mrs. Barton."

Sally Mae looked affronted, her tiny fist clenched at her side, her head held high. "This is Eagle Rock, Mr. Warwick. It's a fortress."

"It's designed to be such," Shane said, nodding his head. "But I have reason to believe your daughter might not be completely protected."

"And I won't put all of you in danger," Kit added, hoping her mother would listen to reason. "If Shane isolates me, then I won't have to worry about everyone else."

Sally Mae shut the door then put her hands on her hips. "Are you telling me you think someone on the inside is behind this? We've been through that already with Devon and Lydia, remember? And with Eli and Gena. That was definitely an inside job from one of our top operatives. But he's dead and gone and I thought it was over. Mercy, when will it end?"

Shane touched a hand to her arm. "I'm not saying that. I don't believe this threat is coming from within CHAIM ranks. We've pretty much wiped that problem clean. But I do worry that someone from the outside knows Katherine is here. And that's why I think it best to take her to an undisclosed location where few people are—the fewer people involved the better."

Sally Mae's shrewd gaze passed over his face. "You're one of the best, I'll give you that. But you can't take her out of here without discussing this with my husband."

Shane let out a breath. "You know that will only delay things. I don't have time to listen to a lecture or to go over strategy by committee. My gut is telling me to get your daughter to safety immediately and worry about the details later."

"But—"

"Mother, I'm not a prisoner here," Kit said, using her best assertive voice. "I can leave on my own or you can let the man you hired to protect me do his job. And you can try trusting me. I won't be responsible for someone doing harm to anyone inside Eagle Rock or out."

Sally Mae clutched at her gold rope necklace. "I declare, I don't know about you young folks. We had a way of doing things back in the day, but now…"

"Now threats can come from many sources," Shane said, glancing over at Katherine. "If I can get her to a safe location, I can do some digging and get to the bottom of this. Starting with Jacob's death and working from there."

Sally Mae gasped. "Are you saying there was more to that? I knew it. I tried to tell your daddy—" She stopped, her expression thoughtful. Finally she said, "Okay, what's the plan?"

Kit heard Shane's exhaled breath. Had he been planning to take her hostage as he'd suggested earlier if her mother refused to cooperate?

"The first order of business is a means of getting us out of here," Shane said. "We need a car."

Sally Mae nodded. "I can help with that. We've got plenty of vehicles around here. Meet me in the garage in about five minutes." She turned to Kit. "Are you sure, honey?"

Kit didn't want to lie to her mother. She wasn't sure but she couldn't risk getting all of them killed. "I don't have any other choice right now, Mother. It's best if I distance myself from all of you—to protect you."

"And what about you?" Sally Mae asked.

"Shane will take care of me."

Sally Mae turned toward the door then whirled toward Shane. "You listen to me, and listen good. If anything happens to my daughter…well, you just remember I was once a CHAIM agent myself and I still know a few surefire ways of dealing with those who fail me—or make me mad."

Shane's eyes widened. "I understand, Mrs. Barton. And you have my word I will protect her with my very life."

"That's mighty reassuring," her mother replied with all of the serenity and sweetness of someone at a country club luncheon. "Now, about that car…"

"A yellow Miata?"

Shane stared down at the toy car sitting in front of him, not sure he could get his legs to fit in the tiny thing, let alone his entire body. Even with the top down, he didn't see how he could be comfortable, but he didn't dare put the top down tonight.

Sally Mae shoved the keys at him. "Look, it's the only one I can spare right now. It's little, it's fast and it's bulletproof. Even the hard top, which I suggest you don't let down. You'd be like low-hanging fruit with the top down. And it gets good gas mileage." She shrugged. "What more could you want?"

"A real car," Shane said on a snort. "This is like a go-cart on steroids."

"Take it or leave it," Sally Mae replied. "The SUVs all have the standard CHAIM GPS tracking." She lifted her eyebrows. "Which means—"

"That your husband could track us, I know, I know," Shane interrupted. "And you're sure this car isn't bugged?"

"No, it is not," Sally Mae replied, her indignation showing in the flash in her eyes. "It has a GPS system, of course. But that's just so I can find where I'm going when I'm shopping or lunching, you know. Woman-type stuff. I like my privacy and my husband knows I can dislodge any tracking system in about five minutes, anyway. So he indulges me now and then."

"By allowing you to drive around in a bright yellow car that looks like a bumblebee?" Shane asked.

"Hey, it's cute and it's fast—I had the engine reworked to make it a little quicker," she replied. "And you're wasting time."

"You're right," Shane said, looking over at Kit. "Get in."

Sally Mae patted the little car. "Oh, and just so you know, it does have an emergency button. That red one on the dash. Hit that and you'll get a secure satellite line right back to Eagle Rock. Or you can request a secure line to signal any other agent by code."

"Good to know," Shane said, impressed with Sally Mae's steel magnolia calm. He handed her Kit's cell. "We won't need this. She's to have no contact with anyone for the next few days, understand?"

Kit didn't like that. "No contact? But I have obligations, calls to return. Everyone will be wondering where I am."

"We'll take care of all that, honey," her mother replied, holding the phone up in the air.

Kit had remained quiet while her mother and Shane discussed their mode of transportation. But now, he saw the apprehension in her eyes. "Katherine?"

"I'm ready," she said, turning to her mother. "I love you."

Sally Mae pulled her daughter into her tiny arms, hugging Kit close with a mother's fierce protection. "I'll stall your daddy. He'll be madder than a hornet but it won't be the first time I've made him mad." She looked at Shane, her expression bordering on murder to him while she said such sweet words to her child. "I love you, honey, and I expect all of this to be over real soon. You have my prayers."

Shane interpreted that look to mean "And I expect you to keep her safe or you will have to answer to me, Mister."

He nodded to Sally Mae and she silently accepted that nod as his promise. Then she stood back to look up at Katherine. "This life isn't for sissies, that's for sure. We've tried to do good over the years but sometimes bad catches up to us. It's warfare, honey. Always. But we have to fight the good fight, no matter what."

Katherine kissed her mother again then slipped with lady-like agility into the low car, leaving Shane to shove her designer overnight bag into the small trunk.

"Thank you, Mrs. Barton," he said as he opened the door. "I won't forget your help."

Sally Mae waved a hand in dismissal. "You can thank me by finding out who's behind this and bringing my daughter home safely. Now I'll open the gate and then I have some explaining to do to my husband."

"Of course," Shane said, praying that he could deliver on his promises.

Then he forced himself into the tiny space behind the wheel, cranked the little car and listened to the purring motor for a few seconds before he shifted gears and took off into the night.

"Where are we going?" Kit asked after they cleared the gates of the sprawling complex and hit the main highway.

Shane didn't want to talk about it. The less she knew, the safer she'd be. But he understood her need for answers. "Remember the ranch I mentioned near Fort Worth? My father's ranch? Mine now."

"You're taking me there?"

He nodded. "It's big and vast. And secluded. The isolation will give me time to focus on research and give you time to unwind so you can answer some specific questions for me."

"About my husband?"

He'd have to remember she was a very smart woman. "Yes, that and other things. Something, someone that can trigger memories that might give us some clues."

"Jacob and I met in college. I fell for him instantly. He was smart, ambitious and he believed in all the causes I wanted to support. It was as if he'd been hand-picked to find me. I decided God had put him in my life for a purpose."

"So you left school and became his wife?"

"Yes. My senior year. Jacob wanted us to be married right away. I always wanted to go back and get my degree, but you know how that goes."

"You got busy with your life and then Jacob practiced law and moved up the ladder in politics."

"Yes. We both had connections, so we used that clout to get him elected. He was a very smart man and people listened to him, believed in him. He was good for Texas."

Shane kept his eyes on the road. "Tell me about your life before Jacob."

She smiled at that, memories darting through her mind like a child running through a field. "I had a good life. My parents loved me, loved God and taught me to always do the right thing. I wanted to serve others. Not in a Mother Teresa way, of course. But I wanted to do what I could to help people. After I married Jacob, I had that chance. The foundation supports several global charities."

"Such as?"

She saw the spark of interest in his eyes. "Shane, the foundation is solid. And clean."

"Such as?" he asked again, never skipping a beat.

"We do work with orphans in the Middle East. We support a school down in a remote village in Mexico. We work with school children here in Texas to improve grade scores and prevent dropout rates from going up. And we've started a new program on environmental issues."

He glanced in the rearview mirror. "I have the list of your board of directors. I might need to glance over that again with you, see if any one name stands out."

"Most of our board members are pillars of society."

"That doesn't mean they're perfect, luv."

"I can't see anyone on our board wanting to harm me."

"We have to keep digging."

When he looked in the mirror a second time, then checked the side mirrors, Kit grew uneasy. "Is something wrong?"

"Maybe," he said, his brow furrowing. "I think someone is following us." She tried to turn, but he grabbed her shoulder. "Don't look back."

Thinking they'd had a brief reprieve, she said, "What are we going to do?"

Shane checked the mirrors again then smiled. "We're going to put your mother's adorable little car to the test. We're going to outrun them, of course."

And then he hit the gas and blasted the little car off so quickly, Kit had to hold onto the dashboard. "I guess taking this car wasn't very smart, was it?"

"It's all right," he replied. "It's bulletproof remember?"

Kit nodded, but she wondered if that would help them now. She wasn't sure if anything could help them at this point. She leaned her head back against the tiny black leather headrest, dread gripping her.

Shane exited the road and waited. When the other car kept to the main road, he patted her hand. "False alarm, but I'm going to take the back road, just in case."

Watching him shift into reverse, she said, "So you think whoever this is might be from my husband's past?"

"It's a good place to start. If that helicopter crash wasn't an accident, then someone deliberately set out to kill Jacob. And now they're coming after you.

Which means they think you know something or have something that they don't want you to have."

"But it's been a whole year since my husband died and I can't imagine what they think I know."

"They probably watched you for a few months to find clues and when you did nothing, they went into action. Or your recent activities, something you did or said, inadvertently tipped them off, got their attention. They'd dig into your daily life and routine so they could form a plan based on your activities. Some of the threats you received were more in the form of intimate questions, coming from various quarters. People were being a bit too pushy in asking about your personal history. Then you started receiving those pointed phone calls and obvious intrusions in your office and possibly your home, so they must have found something to scare them into a bold attempt."

"Oh, well, that explains why they waited until I was inside a packed ballroom with all kinds of civic leaders and prominent people from all over Texas, right?"

He touched a hand to hers. "They might have had more than one target tonight, Katherine. First, you. Then…who knows. That's why it's imperative we find out what's going on."

She pulled her hand away, shock slicing across the shadows over her face. "It's worse than I imagined. You mean they could *still* come after my parents, my friends, and my staff?"

"I can't be sure, but yes. Removing you from the situation could bring them out of hiding, at least."

"And cause someone else to become the target? No!" She thrashed around, grabbing at his arm. "Shane, turn this car around now!"

He held her off with one hand while he steered the car with the other. "It's not like that. It's complicated."

"Complicated?" Her laughter was tinged with disbelief. "You can say that again. First, you tell me I'm the one in danger and now, after you force me to leave with you, you're telling me others might still be targets, too? How can I trust anything you say to me?"

Shane let go of her and focused on the road. "Can you trust that *you* are my number one priority? Can you trust that getting you away from Eagle Rock was the first line of defense?"

She shook her head. "But my parents?"

"They will be safe. Your father knows how to deal with this sort of thing. And your mother seems very capable of taking care of herself, too."

That bit of levity seemed to calm her a bit. She pushed at her hair then stared out the window. "What about all the others? Who's going to protect them?"

"Already taken care of," he said. "Your father and I agreed immediately after the shooting that we'd need to put people on those closest to you. Your staff is being watched and so are your closest friends."

"Including Trudy?"

"Especially Trudy," he replied, his tone never belying the fact that Katherine's best friend was a person of interest in this entire case.

FIVE

Dawn was rising in a burst of orange and yellow pastels behind them when Shane pulled the little car off the main highway and onto a clay road that trailed around a low valley surrounded by wooded hills. "We're almost there."

Kit glanced over at him, wondering how she'd gone from a glittering charity ball in the heart of the city to being on the run in a Miata with an Englishman she didn't even know. "You weren't kidding when you said it was off the beaten path."

His brow wrinkled into a grim frown. "Purposely so. My father liked his privacy. This place is secluded and hard to find. And I like it that way, too."

Kit looked toward the beamed gate where a tiny sign was the only indication that they'd reached the ranch. "*Rancho solo del Roble*. Lonely Oak Ranch." Had he brought her to the end of the earth?

Shane hit a button on his fancy phone and waited for the gates to swing open. Then he pointed up the long lane.

"Lonely Oak," he said, showing Kit the towering old live oak that greeted them as they came around the curve in the open field. The scarred, aged tree branched out with mushroom-shaped symmetry like a welcoming shelter toward the sky. "That tree has been here for over three hundred years. It's my compass toward home."

She filed that away in her good-to-know mental notebook, along with all the prayers she'd gone over in her head tonight. So the formidable, world-weary Sir Shane Warwick did have a home. And in the middle of the Lone Star state, of all places. "You come here a lot then?"

"As often as I can, between assignments. This place keeps me grounded. It's a good place for prayer and contemplation. It's so different from the stuffy old rooms at Warwick Hall—which used to be called something else until my mother married my father and they inherited the place. My father's ego couldn't allow it to be called anything but Warwick, of course."

Kit heard the hint of resentment in Shane's voice. "Were you close to your father?"

He nodded but kept the frown. "As close as a father and son can be, I suspect. We had our clashes, of course. I attended all the right schools in England but my father insisted I come here for my real education. I learned a lot about life on this old ranch. And then, he introduced me to your father and his…er…friends."

"You mean, your father suggested you join the ranks of CHAIM?"

"Strongly suggested," he shot back. "And I have to admit, I was hooked from the first orientation seminar. I wanted to serve God and help other human beings. Plus, I get to play with all sorts of cool gadgets."

"And how's that working for you so far?"

He smiled at that, his gaze lingering on her. "It has its moments."

Kit viewed the rolling hills as they neared the ranch house, her gaze taking in more oaks as well as elm trees and a pecan grove. Off in a far pasture, massive long-horns strolled over the grassy fields. She could picture Shane here sitting on a big horse, galloping through the pastures. But that image made him a paradox.

"You were caught between two worlds and now you're caught in a dark, secret world."

"Yes, I was caught," he replied, apparently choosing to ignore her pointed comment about his current occupation. "A proper young Englishman who knew the decorum of having royal blood flowing in my veins—my mother saw to that—and the youth yearning to break free and just live my life. And my father taught me that, in more ways than I wanted to know, I'm afraid. CHAIM has taught me the rest."

Kit watched his face, saw so many flickering emotions etched there in the crinkles at his eyes, in the tanned slashes of his jaw. What had he seen or done in the name of CHAIM? And did she dare tell him she'd had those same conflicting emotions about breaking free and just becoming herself? Probably not. Not now at least.

He slowed the car and downshifted. "We're almost there."

Kit dropped her dark thoughts and looked up to find a sprawling two-storied Spanish type stucco ranch house similar to Eagle Rock sitting atop a tree-shaded hill. But where Eagle Rock was all modern sophistication, this house set in another time. Obviously, it had been built long ago and updated through the years. Beyond the house and stables a creek bed gurgled through the pasture.

"The house is stunning," she said. "And the creek is beautiful."

"That creek flows toward the Brazo River," Shane explained. "Plenty of good bass fishing. We have long-horns in the pastures and whitetail deer roaming the meadows at dusk. Plus lots of other creatures."

Kit shuddered involuntarily at that, her reasons for being here once again front and center in her mind. "Under normal circumstances, I think I'd love this place. But we're not here for a vacation."

"No, we're not," he said, shifting the car forward. Driving around toward the back of the house, he looked over at her. "First things first. You need to rest." As if sensing her trepidation about being here with him in such a secluded place, he added, "We have a staff of three—very loyal and very trustworthy. And my grand-mother lives here year-round."

Kit's shock registered in her words. "Your grand-mother? You have a grandmother?"

"Yes, and as I said, she lives here as part of the staff but she doesn't have to work as hard as the rest of us, of course. So you have an *abuela*. That should make you feel better about things."

"She's your grandmother, not mine," Kit countered with a soft smile. "What if she doesn't like having me here?"

"Abuela?" He laughed, his eyes crinkling. "She loves everyone. And she'll spoil you, too."

"So she's your father's mother?"

"Something like that. She's not his biological mother, but she raised him from a young age after my real grand-mother died. So that makes her as close to a grandmother as I can have. My grandparents are long dead—on both sides."

Kit was beginning to understand why he was a nomad, a man who couldn't settle down. "I see. So you 'adopt' people, so to speak?"

He brought the car up to a big garage attached to a long, covered gallery toward the main house. A big pickup and a couple of off-road vehicles were parked inside. "I suppose I do. I have a lot of good friends all over the world."

But he hadn't mentioned anyone in particular, such as a special woman in his life. Had he ever brought another woman here, she wondered? She almost asked then decided against it. She wasn't here as a special friend. She was here because someone was after her.

But Kit did wonder if she'd be counted among his friends once this was all over. She could see that Shane was a loyal, devout person. He'd do his job, no matter the cost. But at the end of his assignment, would he disappear back into that dark, murky world that being a CHAIM operative demanded? Would she ever see him again?

Remembering the way she'd reached up and taken his hand last night, she wondered why she held that hope so high. The man was her hired bodyguard. Nothing more—no matter how he made her heart lurch and shift in the same way he'd made this sweet little car purr through the dark night. He'd managed to bring them here in less than the three hours it normally took from Austin to hit the Fort Worth city limits about fifty miles behind them. He might also manage to move with swift expertise into her heart, too. If she let him.

She couldn't depend on a man who could be packed

and ready to move on in thirty minutes. She didn't even want to depend on any man right now. She still missed her husband. And prayed she'd one day be able to let Jacob go.

"Kit?"

She looked up from her silent prayers to find Shane's crystal blue eyes centered on her. "What?"

"Let's get you inside. You're exhausted."

She didn't argue with him on that point. She was numb with a bone-deep tiredness that made it hard to lift out of the low-seated car.

So Shane came around and lifted her up, his arms holding her waist for just a few seconds too long before he turned and got her bag out of the trunk. "Come on. Let's get you settled."

Kit doubted she'd ever be settled again.

Abuela Silvia clicked and clucked over Kit like a mother hen while Shane made a few calls on his secure cell phone and then instructed the staff regarding their houseguest.

"Mrs. Atkins is under my protection, so be aware of that and follow proper protocol. She is to be given every consideration," he said in both English and Spanish, his tone gentle but assertive. "Make her comfortable and let her rest for as long as she needs today."

Abuela Silvia nodded, waving an aged hand in the air toward her grandson, Ricardo. "Go, go. Back to work now."

Ricardo did as his grandmother asked, while his mother Nina just smiled over at Kit. "It's good to have you with us, Mrs. Atkins. I'll show you to your room."

"Let me have a look at things first, Nina," Shane said, hurrying ahead of them toward the gleaming wrought-iron and wood staircase that dominated one corner of the tiled entryway. "Just as a precaution," he said to Kit, his hand on her back.

Kit didn't respond. She looked drained and disoriented. And how could he blame the woman? She'd been snatched away in the night, taken from the people she loved and brought to this beautiful but desolate place for her own protection. She was in shock.

Shane went into the big bedroom located in the middle of the top floor, his hands touching on vases and lamps, his eyes scanning the walls for any signs of unseen visitors. This ranch was his haven, his safe retreat. He knew in his heart no one had been here but he had to be sure. He'd do an entire sweep of the house later, run a few scans on the computerized security system. That would make him feel better. He felt sure they hadn't been followed and he'd taken every precaution to make sure no one had tailed them. And still he worried.

He turned to find Kit and Nina standing at the doorway, silent and watchful. Nina was used to this but even though Kit had grown up with this type of paranoia, she didn't need to worry about it right now.

"I think things are fine," he said to Nina. "Will you help Mrs. Atkins get ready for a nap?"

"Of course." The dark-haired woman who'd lost her husband to the war in the Middle East took Kit by the arm. "Let me show you where everything is, ma'am."

"It's Kit," Kit replied with a soft smile.

Always with the impeccable manners, Shane noticed. Even when she was dead-tired on her feet.

"I'll leave you to it then," he said to Nina, but his eyes held Kit's. "If you need me, use the phone by your bed and hit Operator. It works like an intercom throughout the house."

She nodded, her eyes holding his. Eyes full of questions and doubts, eyes too beautiful to be so sad and unsure. "Thank you."

Shane hoped she'd sleep. She needed rest.

And he needed to sit down and figure out where to begin in trying to find out who wanted her dead.

Shane wasted no time getting down to business. After some strong coffee and a ham biscuit Abuela Silvia insisted he eat, he went into his study at the back of the house and clicked on his laptop. Then he put in a call to Kissie Pierre in New Orleans. The longtime CHAIM operative was the go-to girl for digging up information no one else could find. While Kissie ran a halfway house for troubled teens and managed a coffeehouse on the premises of the old French Quarter mansion where she lived, she also continued to work behind the scenes for CHAIM.

"Shane Warwick. What a surprise," Kissie said, her throaty chuckle making Shane think of warm gumbo and buttered cornbread. "I've heard some chatter about you, Knight."

"I'm sure you have," Shane responded, his own smile belying his concern. "What did you hear?"

"That you brought down some assassin right in the middle of a posh Austin charity ball then somehow managed to take Katherine Barton Atkins right out of the gates of Eagle Rock with Gerald Barton in the house."

"A bit overblown, but accurate," Shane said, pinching his nose with two fingers. "What's the real word?"

He could hear her shuffling papers. Then he heard computer keys singing. "The official word—in the papers and on the news—a would-be burglar tried to rob some of your clients' rich friends during a fund-raiser party at a big downtown hotel. As the story goes, an unknown security officer hired by the Barton Atkins Foundation brought the burglar down without killing him or hurting a single guest. You're a hero. An unknown hero since the press can't seem to locate you."

"And the authorities have been briefed to keep it that way," Shane replied. "Hopefully, it will die down and I can get on with finding out who's trying to harm our beautiful subject."

"Yes, the cover is that Mrs. Atkins is in seclusion for her own protection—just until the authorities can clear her to return to her duties within the organization. Reports indicate she was scheduled for some big mission trip to Mexico in a month or so."

Shane's antenna went up on that one. "Dig into that a bit more, will you, luv? And in the meantime, I'll get back to my job here."

"And have you figured out that job yet? Or did you just decide to spend some downtime with a beautiful blonde?"

Shane admired Kissie's no-nonsense attitude. She was street smart and full of soul. But she believed in CHAIM and she worked hard to keep kids off the streets of New Orleans, so he could deal with her wry sense of humor.

"I'm about to get started on that very thing—the job that is. The beautiful blonde is resting right now."

Kissie whistled low. "You know, Knight, you don't do so great with pretty women. They tend to make you lose your focus. Maybe I should take over this case."

The teasing in her words didn't hide the bit of warning in her tone. Kissie was ever the moral compass of the whole CHAIM team but she sure had him pegged. "Are you suggesting I'll let a beautiful Austin widow go to my head, dear Kissie?"

"You've been known to fall fast and hard before, yeah."

"But Kissie, you know you have my heart," he retorted, hoping to deflect her warnings and the memories they brought up. "I'll be on my best behavior, I can assure you. Gerald Barton would have me tarred and feathered if I dared make a move on his lovely daughter."

"You can count on that, anyway," Kissie replied. "The man is spitting mad, especially since you've blocked all of his alerts and refuse to report in. Yep, you sure got it bad."

"I know exactly what I'm doing," Shane replied, calm in spite of Kissie's dire warnings. "She wasn't safe there. And you can put that in the report that I'm sure you'll send directly to Mr. Barton when you're finished with me."

"I'm just saying," Kissie replied. "But enough with your love life or this death wish you seem to have. What do you need from me?"

"A bit of research for starters. The initial threats started about two months ago—just some odd e-mail inquiries and too many questions regarding her travel

schedule—from sources her organization couldn't iden-
tify. Then she got some strange phone calls, threatening
her and warning her to stick close to home. I need to
set up a timeline of all of Mrs. Atkins' activities beginning the year before her husband died and leading up
to the present. Her travels abroad, all the organizations
she's worked for or served on as a board member and
any new contacts she made in the past few months, that
sort of thing. Especially anything you can find on her
upcoming trip to Mexico."

"Her life history," Kissie said, already tapping her
fingers on the keyboard. "Give me a little time. I'll post
it when it's ready."

"Thank you," Shane said. "And in the meantime, I'll
do a search of any radical groups in Texas—for starters.
I'm thinking someone didn't approve of State Senator
Jacob Atkins. If I can find something, some indiscretion
in his past, I might be able to trace that back to why
someone is trying to kill his widow."

"Got it," Kissie said. "I'll see if I stumble on anything
on this end."

"Thanks again," Shane said. "You have my heart."

"And you have a way with words, even if I don't
believe anything you say," Kissie replied. "You'll hear
from me soon."

"Oh, Kissie, before you go—who's playing in the
coffeehouse tonight?"

She laughed at that. "Still love your jazz, Warwick?"

"I do," he said, "but I like my country songs, too."

"Then you'd love this gig tonight. Southern style
blues—a bit of country and a bit of Mississippi Delta
with a little gospel thrown in for good measure."

"Ah, wish I could be there."

"Come on down when you get done with this case. I'll have 'em back in just for you."

"I might take you up on that offer."

Shane cleared the phone screen then stared at the computer, wondering where he should start. Did he dare go through the CHAIM archives to see if Katherine's father had past dealings with his son-in-law, Jacob Atkins? Couldn't hurt. By his way of thinking, everyone around Katherine Barton Atkins was suspect right now.

Especially those closest to her.

SIX

Kit woke abruptly to find the sun setting behind the hills to the west. Disoriented, she sat up and glanced around the big comfortable room, remembering she wasn't in her lonely house back in Austin. Nor was she at Eagle Rock in the bedroom where they always put their charges—the cause of the month—she thought bitterly.

"Now I'm one of those," she said out loud, her voice croaking and raw. All of her life, she'd known and understood that her father was involved in a highly secretive security company that helped Christians in their time of need. But she'd never dreamed she'd be on the run and in need of the exclusive services CHAIM offered to people. Which brought to mind—was this coincidence or was she a target because of her father's line of work?

Deciding she didn't have the energy to consider the answer to that nagging question, she thought about Shane and how solicitous he'd been to her. Just one more thing she had to adjust to—Shane Warwick in her life. She certainly never imagined she'd be holed up in a beautiful old Spanish-style mansion somewhere west of Fort Worth with a British operative called The Knight, a man who personified all of the stereotypes she'd read about in books or watched on the movie screen.

Personified, yes. Outshined completely, double yes. The real live man she'd been forced to rely on was much better than any fictional character or screen star. Shane had immediately taken control of a scary situation last night. He'd not only saved her; he'd also saved everyone in that room. And for that she'd be forever thankful.

Sir Shane Warwick was the real deal. A real life security expert and spy who'd signed on to protect her. And he was also an interesting, intriguing man who moved through several different worlds with grace and assurance. She had yet to see him ruffled or distracted. That gave her a feeling of security in spite of her worries.

Lifting her hands then letting them fall by her side, she looked up at the intricate gold-etched arched ceiling over the bed. "Couldn't you have sent a different man, maybe someone with a paunch and a balding head?"

If she weren't so terrified, she'd have to laugh out loud. But nothing about this was funny.

Katherine got up and wobbled around the room. She was sore from her head to her toes, probably from tense muscles and holding on for dear life for the last twenty-four hours. "Just breathe," she told herself as she wandered around in constant prayer, her hand touching on the wrought iron of the bedposts, her gaze taking in the beautiful portrait over the marble fireplace of a dark-haired *senorita* astride a great white horse. "Exquisite," she whispered, thinking Sir Shane Warwick wouldn't accept anything less.

And yet even if he had been knighted by the queen, he seemed a simple man, a simple man who knew how to dress and how to use a weapon, she mused as she went into the adjourning bathroom and almost wept with delight over the beautiful soaking tub and rainforest-like shower.

After washing her face, she turned to find a set of clothes laid out on a pretty brocade chair near a large closet. Noting that the jeans and sweater were her own—or ones she'd taken from Eagle Rock, Katherine went about freshening up—a long shower followed by a bit of makeup. Then she stopped and said a few more prayers, part of her usual morning ritual.

Fully dressed, she realized she was starving. The kitchen. She'd find her way to the kitchen and make herself a good strong cup of coffee and a grilled cheese.

She made it out into the hallway before she was stopped with two strong hands on her arm.

"What are you doing?"

Katherine looked up to find Shane staring down at her, his expression shadowed, his eyes blazing hot.

"Hello to you, too," she said, her breath hitching in her throat. Did he have to appear so sinister and so concerned all in one fell swoop? And he was just as dashing in jeans, a button-down shirt and boots as in a tuxedo.

He stepped back, surveying her as if she were some sort of interloper, until his eyes went soft and steely blue. "Did you rest?"

"I did. I must have slept all day, since the sun's going down and my stomach is growling for dinner."

"Good. I was on my way to check on you. Dinner is ready."

Katherine wondered just how many times he'd checked on her during the day. Knowing him, she figured he'd been sitting out here by her door for hours.

"Then I'm right on time, aren't I?" she asked, her smile hiding the unease that had settled on her like a yoke and refused to let go. "What are we having?"

"Spicy lime chicken, I believe," he said, turning to guide her toward the stairs. Then he leaned close. "Don't leave your room again without notifying me first, okay?"

Katherine stopped at the top of the stairs, a mural along the stairway of a courtyard lush with forest green ferns and rich pink bougainvillea blossoms acting as a backdrop to his reprimand. "Am I a prisoner here, Shane?"

His gaze swept her in that way that left her slightly dazed. "No, you're under my protection. And that means I need to know where you are twenty-four/seven. All you have to do is pick up the phone and alert either the staff or me each time you leave your room."

"If I'm safe here, then why the need for all this?" she asked, knowing the answer before he grabbed her arm to halt her.

"You're safe for now," he said, his eyes glazed with aggravation. "But someone is after you, Katherine. We have to take every precaution."

"Isn't that why you brought me here?"

He held her there on the stairs, his expression at once hostile and hopeful. "Yes. This place is so off the beaten path, I doubt anyone can find us. But—"

"But these people, whoever they are, might be able to do just that, right?" Yanking her hand away, she took off down the stairs. "Maybe I should have stayed at Eagle Rock."

"Maybe you should have," he said after her, taking

the stairs at a run to catch up with her. "Do you want me to take you back?"

She whirled in the dining room. "What? We just got here."

"But if you're not pleased with the accommodations…"

Not sure if she'd truly offended him or he was just testing her to make sure she understood how things had to be, she went straight to the Rococo buffet table and helped herself to a steaming cup of coffee from the silver urn. "The accommodations are beautiful and your staff is very considerate. But your boorish way of bossing me around is irritating. Especially when I just woke up."

Shane stomped to the buffet and poured a glass of water then drank the whole thing down. "Excuse me for trying to keep you alive."

That statement halted her and caused Ricardo, who'd just entered the arched doorway from the kitchen with a steaming bowl of rice, to whirl and exit the same way he'd entered.

Katherine turned to glare at Shane across the long room. She started to speak but shut her mouth. Then she took a long sip of her coffee and closed her eyes for a minute. When she opened them, she smiled serenely at him. "I'm sorry. This is difficult, Shane. You've done everything possible to help me and I'm being a brat. Please bear with me and let me get adjusted. I think I just needed some caffeine."

He lowered his head, his gaze following her as she sniffed at the food spread out on the buffet. "I understand. You're not used to being closed off from the world."

"No, I'm not," she said, motioning toward the spicy-smelling chicken. "Can we eat while we talk?"

"Of course." Shane followed her along the buffet, taking meat and vegetables onto his plate with aggravated efficiency. He waited for her to sit, then took his seat across from her at the long table. "I apologize for my testiness. I've been poring over documents all afternoon."

Kit sat down, flipped her linen napkin open then began to cut her chicken into little bite-size pieces. "Documents about me?"

Ricardo made another effort to deliver the rest of their dinner, entering with his head down and his stride full of purpose. After he placed the dishes on the buffet, Shane nodded to the boy then waved a hand for him to leave the room.

His frown answered Kit's question however. Then he asked another one. "You travel a great deal, don't you?"

She sent a glowering look right back at him. "That's part of my job at the foundation. I don't like sitting back while others do all the work."

"You've put yourself on the line, traveling to some of the most dangerous spots on earth."

"Unfortunately, those spots are also the most needy."

He took a long sip of iced tea. "That puts you in a very compromising position—your face is all over the Internet and in every major newspaper in the world."

"My face gets me the publicity I need to fund my causes, Shane."

"And also makes you an easy target for criminals."

She dropped her fork. "Did you find something?"

He sat back against the studded burgundy leather seat of the high-backed mahogany chair. "Oh, yes. I found out everything I'd ever want to know about Katherine Barton Atkins. You've had dealings with so many heads of state, it makes my brain fuzzy."

Trying to picture this brooding man with a fuzzy brain made her smile inside. But she didn't dare smile at him right now. She needed to be as cooperative as possible.

"So what do we do now?" she asked, ready to get down to business.

After connecting some of the dots that made up her busy, highly public life, Shane wondered that himself. "We wait." He chewed his own chicken, the taste of fresh jalapeños complementing the tangy lime in the juicy, tender chicken. His ulcer would protest this later. "I've done some research, sent out some feelers."

"Regarding?"

Regarding a few of the trips she'd taken over the last months and the one she planned to take later this fall. But he wouldn't tell her that. Nor would he tell her that he was a bit concerned that her friend Trudy Pearson seemed to have gone underground, too, since the authorities in Austin couldn't reach her for further questioning. Maybe Trudy was still frightened after last night's shoot-out. That was reasonable, but his burning stomach made him wonder.

"Regarding your life," he said to Kit. "I need to piece things together. And now that you're rested, maybe you can help. Let's start with your upcoming trip to Mexico. Why were you going there?"

"You mean, why *am* I going there? I fully intend

to make that trip. We're taking medical supplies to a remote village and we're going to help finish building the clinic several organizations have been working on for over two years now. "Our trip will be the last one. We'll hold a large celebration there once we're finished."

"Very high profile."

"Yes, to get the much-needed attention of leaders in both of our countries."

"Did your husband ever go down there with you?"

She seemed wary then nodded. "A couple of times, yes."

"And did he ever conduct any other business while there?"

"No, why would he? He helped us. He volunteered as much as he could—when he wasn't on the phone with his staff back home. And speaking of that, I should alert my staff," she said, her hand steady on her water glass. "They'll be worried."

"Already done. They understand you're a bit traumatized by what happened last night. We have the weekend to tidy this up before people start asking questions."

"My cell phone—"

"Has been taken away for your own protection. Your staff has been advised to make no calls for now. And we're monitoring all incoming calls."

"And my parents?"

"Know you're safe with me."

"How did my father take our quick exit?"

"Not very well." He had to grin at that even though she'd managed to steer the conversation away from her husband and Mexico. "I called in earlier and…let's just say he wasn't very appreciative of my tactic, but he's a bit calmer now that he knows my purpose. Still, I think I'm in hot water."

"Well then, welcome to my world," she said, holding up her glass in salute. "I've been in trouble with that man for most of my life."

Shane could only image how a father such as Gerald Barton would do anything to protect his only child. And perhaps smother her to the point of exhaustion, too. "Does your father have a forgiving nature?"

Her chuckle rattled with dryness. "He wasn't exactly thrilled when I left college to marry Jacob."

Antennas went off inside Shane's brain. He'd read about that, too. Seen the elaborate wedding pictures. She made a lovely bride. And the whole union had read like a perfect power match, something all Texans with old money lived for. "Oh, why is that? Wanted you to have a degree to fall back on?"

She crinkled her nose. "It wasn't the degree. He didn't want me to marry Jacob Atkins." Her words were so full of bitterness that it seemed to shock even her. She actually blushed, looking flustered for a few seconds before she regained that regal control, her hand grasping at her pearls. "It doesn't really matter now, though, does it?"

Shane needed to know more because it might matter a whole lot. He'd never picked up on any disapproval in all the news reports. But then, everyone would have been on their best behavior for the press. "So your father didn't approve of your husband? Interesting." Even more interesting that Gerald hadn't shared this bit of information. But then, it was a family matter and private.

She looked up at him, her eyes turning wary again. "It's hard to explain but I can assure you, it's nothing sinister. They disagreed on some of the issues regarding an oil-and-gas merger between Barton Industries and the company Jacob worked for at the time. He was the attorney in charge of the merger. But they worked it out between them and after we got married, they became close. Jacob and I had a few good years together, in spite of everything."

Shane didn't press her to explain that "in spite of everything" ending since he hadn't found anything incriminating regarding her father's dealings with Jacob. But he would have to revisit the merger she just mentioned. He watched as she shut back down, her expression going soft and uniform, trained. And he imagined she'd practiced just such a stance many times with her parents and with the press. Maybe with her husband.

And then a new thought occurred to him.

What was Katherine Atkins hiding from the world?

An hour later, Shane took her out into the secluded courtyard between the house and the garage. Katherine noticed more intricate wrought iron out here on the gates and woven into the heavy stucco walls surrounding the tiled floor of the enclosed patio. A tiered water fountain gurgled in the center, its colorful mosaic tiles shimmering like jewels in the moonlight.

"This looks like the mural by the stairs," she said, glad to have a safe topic to discuss. Glad to be away from the ever-increasing unease of her thoughts and her memories.

"It's the same," Shane replied, handing her another cup of coffee to go with the dark chocolate truffles Nina had left on the buffet. "My mother painted the mural based on this courtyard. She loved it here. Still does."

"It is peaceful," Kit said, taking a deep breath. "And, Shane, I do feel safe here."

"Good." He sounded relieved. They sat silently for a few minutes then he said, "You know I'll protect you."

She ignored the little currents shooting throughout her system like fireflies, chalking them up to the luscious chocolates. "It's your job."

"Yes, but it's also an honor to be trusted enough to help you, even if your father wants my head on a platter."

She sipped her coffee and stared at the water spilling over the fountain, watching as a few stray flower blossoms floated across the bubbling waves. "My father is overprotective. He never liked any of the men I dated, so why would he completely trust the man he hired to protect me?"

"Especially when that man went against the CHAIM handbook and broke every rule ever droned into his thick skull."

"There is that," she retorted, holding her cup to keep her hands from shaking. Why did being alone with Shane Warwick make her feel as inadequate and inexperienced as a shy schoolgirl? It seemed she'd forgotten how to carry on a polite, civil conversation.

"You mentioned that your father didn't like Jacob at first? I can't see that he wouldn't. Jacob Atkins had impeccable credentials—an upstanding family heritage that came from old Texas oil money, a law degree from a prominent university and a sharp, business-centered mind. I'm surprised your father didn't tag Jacob to work for CHAIM."

Katherine understood why she'd been so keyed up

and it had nothing to do with how handsome Shane Warwick was or how his silver-blue eyes held hers. Now she understood. He was fishing for answers, the kind she couldn't give him.

"You're interrogating me, aren't you? You really do think Jacob's death has something to do with these people who are after me? What are you insinuating, Shane?"

"Nothing at all. I told you I needed to ask you some questions. It's the only way I can build a case and find out who's after you."

"But are you building a case to help me, or you trying to establish a case against my husband?" Tired and frightened, she set her coffee down on a nearby table then stood up. "Did my father put you up to accusing my husband of some sort of wrongdoing? Did he? He never believed in Jacob, never."

She stopped, realizing she'd said more than she wanted. She'd given him way too much ammunition already.

"I'm tired. I'm going back to my room now."

But Shane was there, holding her arm, forcing her around to look at him. "Your father never suggested that, Katherine. But I have to tell you, everyone is suspect. Everyone you know, everyone you love, anyone and everyone you've ever done business with or associated with. So you might as well search your mind and get ready for the real interrogation. Because as soon as we go inside, I have another thick file to read over—a file all about the people in your life. And I hope I'll find something inside that file that might give me a clue as to what's going on now."

He took her by the arm, half guiding, half dragging

her toward the open doors into the house. "So get used to being interrogated. And keep in mind, it's part of the job."

"That's obvious," she said, anger clouding her logic. "And we all know you'll do that job in order to please my powerful father, no matter how much it might hurt me, right?"

She watched as he gritted his teeth then nodded. "If it means keeping you alive, yes, that's exactly what I'll do. And you'll just have to get over that." Then he tugged her close, his face inches from her own. "But make no mistake, this isn't about pleasing your father. There is much more going on here."

His eyes moved over her face, settling on her lips.

Katherine lost the ability to breathe. She was about to give him a choice retort just to stop herself from doing something crazy such as kissing him, when they heard a rustling in the bushes at the back of the courtyard. A rustling that sent chills down Katherine's spine and caused Shane to push her toward the doors with a hiss of warning. "Inside now. And stay there."

She watched, her heart caught in her throat, as he pulled a gun out of the waistband of his jeans and headed back out into the night. Watched and wished she hadn't been so flippant about her situation or his job.

SEVEN

Shane carefully opened the well-oiled gate and worked his way around the perimeters of the courtyard walls, his eyes adjusting in the moonlight enough to make out shapes and shadows. The motion detectors were on and gleaming bright out into the night, but he couldn't see anyone out there. Leaning against the still-warm mellowed stucco, he didn't dare breathe as he willed himself to be invisible.

He listened, praying Katherine would stay inside and out of the way. His gun by his side and ready, he moved again, taking each footstep in slow motion until he reached the back corner of the long wall. Stopping underneath a bent mesquite tree, he listened.

The night was as still as a ghost town, the wind quiet and sparse, the air dry and heavy with shadows. Then he heard it again, a soft rustling about five feet away.

Without hesitation, he whirled around the corner, his gun raised, his eyes focused. Then he let out a breath of relief.

An armadillo.

Shane stared down the wobbling uncomely creature, a wry smile on his face. "You don't know how close you came to death, little fellow." Picking up a rock, he threw it toward the thick-shelled animal, watching as the armadillo scurried away into the surrounding pastureland.

After making sure the armadillo was the only thing lurking about behind the house, Shane checked the garage and the outbuildings. Everything seemed intact. No sign of human footprints, no sign of tire tracks or any other sort of tracks. No markings of a horse and rider nearby either.

Was he imagining trouble? His spicy dinner hissed its way through his stomach, burning him with a reminder that only added to his apprehension. Hurrying back to the house, he prayed he'd find Katherine and the others safe.

Katherine stood huddled with Ricardo, Nina and Silvia in the dark kitchen. Ricardo had a shotgun slung over his right shoulder, ready to do battle.

"All clear," Shane said on a sigh of relief. "Our nocturnal visitor was only a lowly armadillo on the prowl."

"Thank goodness," Nina said, shaking her head. "Miss Katherine was terrified."

"We all were," Silvia added, eying her grandson. "This one had to be a big man and get his gun." She kissed Ricardo on the cheek, causing the teenager to groan.

"Sorry for the scare," Shane said, his eyes on Katherine. "But we have to be careful."

Ricardo stood up straight. "Want me to patrol tonight, Shane?"

"No, not necessary," Shane said, a hand on the boy's arm. "You have time enough to learn all the CHAIM maneuvers. No need to worry your mother about that now."

Nina gave Shane an appreciative nod. "I agree." Then she turned to her son. "I know you'd do your best to protect us but you're still so young. You'll get your chance in a few more years."

Ricardo's dark eyes lit up even if he did look disappointed. "Yes, *Madre*. I know, I know."

Shane sent them all back to their quarters then looked at Katherine. "Are you all right?"

"I'm fine. I was just concerned for your safety."

His smile turned tipsy. "You were worried about me?"

"Of course." She shrugged prettily. "If something happens to you, I'm stuck here. What would I do? I couldn't bear endangering Ricardo and his family."

Disappointed that she wouldn't pine away for him, Shane motioned toward the big den. "Let's go and sit down so we can talk." After he'd seated her on a high-backed leather chair, he said, "You will immediately call your father if anything happens to me. He'll send someone or come for you himself. Understand?"

"Yes." She studied him for a few seconds. "I can't stay hidden away here forever, Shane. So let's get on with this. I'll tell you anything you want to know."

Surprised at this turn, he said, "That armadillo must have really shaken you."

She shot him a harsh glare. "It wasn't the armadillo. It was the thought that it could have been a human being out there, ready to kill me. Or worse, shoot you."

Shane saw it all there on her face. Katherine wasn't the kind of woman to watch others suffer, especially if they were doing it for her sake. She'd try to end this as quickly as possible so she could get back to her life, but more importantly, to protect everyone else around her.

And possibly, to distance herself from any further close-ness to him. That could make her a bit too reckless.

Trying to lighten the mood, he leaned forward. "So you *were* worried about me."

Her haughty expression didn't quite make it to her troubled eyes. "Yes, I was worried about you. I told you I didn't want you to get killed on my behalf. Satisfied?"

He put a hand to his heart. "Touched."

She leaned forward, too. "Don't be flippant about this, Shane. I might not like being here, but I certainly do appreciate how you've put yourself on the line for me."

"Accepted," he said, not daring to push this particular issue right now. Nor would he mention how close he'd come to kissing her out there in the courtyard. That wouldn't do, not tonight. Maybe not ever. She had to feel the same things he'd been feeling, but they were both avoiding the obvious. This attraction couldn't go anywhere for many reasons.

"Let's get down to business then," he said, taking her to his office at the back of the house.

"Okay." She took the chair across from his desk and sat straight up, as if facing an executioner. "What do you want to know?"

Shane had read through most of the early reports Kissie had e-mailed him with the promise of more to come. He'd printed the pages out so he could memorize what he needed to know and then destroy them. And he'd highlighted some points to go over with Katherine.

Shuffling through the papers, he said, "Your husband was a state senator for two years."

"Yes. He'd planned on running again." She shrugged.

"He'd talked about running for governor on down the road."

"High aspirations."

She looked down at her folded hands, apparently not so thrilled about being first lady of Texas. "He lived and breathed politics. I think that's why he turned my father down about joining up with CHAIM. His heart wasn't in this kind of work. Of course, I didn't want him to join. We both felt we could serve better if he went into politics and I ran the foundation."

He registered the sadness on her face. This business was hard on families, but her storybook life might have been hard on her. To the point that she was hiding more than a widow's loneliness. "But he supported your father's efforts?"

Her gaze locked with Shane's. "Yes, and why would you even ask that?"

"Oh, no particular reason. But some of these news articles indicate they were at odds on some of the issues of this great state. You said they had some differences early on when you started dating Jacob. Your father didn't always agree with your husband's voting record in the Senate. Even after you became Jacob's wife."

Kit lowered her eyes, staring down at her joined hands. "They did like to argue politics, true. But it was always with respect. They agreed to disagree."

She was hiding something there. Shane could tell by the way she lowered her eyes and looked away. But he didn't press her for more information on that. "Did your husband ever talk to you about any other business associates?"

"We talked about a lot of things. We attended certain functions on his behalf many times. But we also attended functions to promote the Barton Atkins Foundation. We always needed extra funding."

"And you knew at all times where that funding was coming from, how it was being provided?"

"Of course I did. I still do. Jacob had to be careful that his campaign contributions never overlapped our fundraising dollars and vice versa for me. Because of all our holdings, we kept meticulous records for that very purpose. What are you suggesting?"

"I'm not suggesting anything. I'm just asking the proper questions. We have to check every avenue. Some of your husband's holdings are a bit convoluted."

Her pupils dilated, irises a brilliant green, throwing him completely off. Was she trying to protect her husband, or did Shane just make her uncomfortable?

"My foundation is solid and completely transparent. I have good people in place to make sure of that, some of them specifically chosen with my father's help in order to safeguard our funding."

So, she was protecting her foundation. From her husband, maybe, or from her husband's questionable activities. Interesting.

"Did your husband ever suggest patrons or donors?"

"Of course he did. I can't believe you're targeting the foundation this way."

"I'm not targeting anyone, Katherine. Just let me finish."

She shifted, crossed her legs then stared at him. "Go on."

He could tell she was uncomfortable. What was she trying so hard to hide? Was she protecting her husband or someone else close to her? Or was he just imagining things?

"Your husband had a lot of holdings—oil and gas mostly. Did he ever deal in any type of government contracts or deal with other countries?"

"No. I mean, not after he became a senator."

"But what if there was something on the side, some sort of deal under the table?"

Katherine stood up, her hands fisted on the table. "I don't understand why you keep going back to Jacob. The man is dead, Shane. And that death was thoroughly investigated and deemed a tragic accident. The authorities didn't find anything suspicious about his business or his associates. Try looking somewhere else, please."

"I know how to dig into places the authorities might not," he said, hating the hurt in her eyes. "Jacob might have been a decent, honest man but even a good man can get caught up in a bad situation."

She reached up her right hand to clutch her pearls. "Not Jacob. He went by the book."

"Okay then. Let's talk about your friends. How long have you known Trudy Pearson?"

She looked shocked and annoyed but she answered the question. "Since grade school. We've had our share of differences, but she's my best friend."

"And she also lost her husband—just a few months before you lost Jacob."

"Yes, and we've helped each other through that."

"Her husband died of a heart attack?"

"Yes, completely natural causes."

He filed that for more research. "And you and she are still close?"

"Yes, obviously. She helps me with the foundation.

She's one of our biggest donors and a regular volunteer around the office. Very devoted."

"I can see that from her generous contributions."

"So she's clear, right? Surely you don't think—"

Shane didn't want to say anything more about Trudy Pearson right now. "As far as I can see, yes, your friend is clear."

"You don't sound so sure."

He didn't dare tell Katherine that her best friend couldn't be located. But Trudy had left the hotel last night with that catering manager, who also couldn't be found. "I can't be sure about anything at this point."

"No, I suppose not." She let out a sigh. "Is this really necessary, to ask about and suspect the people I care about the most?"

"I'm afraid so. The more people we can eliminate the better off we'll be. And we have to start with those closest to you and work our way from there."

"So you've done background checks on everyone who knows me, right? And what have you found?"

This was tricky, trying to question her without giving anything away. "So far, so good. But we have a lot of ground to cover still. Are you tired?"

"No. I could make us some more coffee and find more of that chocolate Nina left for us."

"More chocolate?" He laughed out loud. "For someone with such a slender figure, you sure can pack away the food."

"I'm a Texas girl. We like to eat."

"You must have good genes."

"More like, a fast metabolism. I'm usually too busy to eat most days. I'm sure I'll gain a few pounds before this is over. I'm a stress eater."

"I see. Maybe we can go for a ride tomorrow, if everything looks safe. Take the horses out. I find a good long ride relieves stress for me."

And on horseback, he could look for anything out of the ordinary.

"That might be nice. Do you have a lot of horses here?"

"About a half dozen. Ricardo is great with them. And Nina and Silvia both are excellent horsewomen. When I'm not here, they pretty much run the place."

"What about Nina's husband? How did he die?"

"He was in the army. He died in the Middle East."

"That's tough. So you offered them a home?"

Shane sat back, his hands on his knees. "It was more like they gave me a home. After my parents began living separate lives, my father only brought me here to hunt or fish, to practice my shooting capabilities with every type of weapon known to man. I did a lot of my CHAIM training right here with some of the senior members, under my father's watchful eye. But at the end of the day, I could always find *Abuela* Silvia in the kitchen, waiting to talk to me. She taught me about Christ, about church, about family. I watched her with Nina and later, young Ricardo and after Nina's husband died, I invited them to live here permanently and help me with the place. I've always wished I had that kind of close-knit family."

"Maybe you still can one day."

He looked across at her, his gaze locking with hers as the image of her in a wedding gown floated through his mind. "Maybe so. It's not easy, but when I think about how happy Devon and Lydia are now—"

"Devon Malone? He's retired from CHAIM, right?"

"Yes, after almost getting himself killed. But he and Lydia are so in love."

"My father brags about them all the time. He seems to adore Lydia."

"She is truly a woman of strong faith."

"And I hear even Eli Trudeau has settled down with Devon's sister Gena."

"That was a surprise. And now they're raising Eli's son Scotty and Eli is always bragging about having more children someday." Shane lifted up in his chair. "All very nice, but some of us aren't meant for that kind of domestic bliss."

Her smile shifted into a frown. "I thought I'd have that. I wanted children but it just never happened."

Shane got an image of her holding a baby in her arms. It was such a beautiful torment, he had to clear his throat. "I'm sorry. You'd make a wonderful mother. You've shown that with your humanitarian efforts."

A flush of heat seared her face. "I'll go make that coffee now."

Shane watched her go, aware that they were dancing around so many questions neither of them could ask. Or answer for that matter. He didn't want to probe into her past. He wanted to hold her close and ask her about the here and now and the future.

And in spite of his declaration to the contrary about domesticity, he wouldn't mind at all being a part of that future. But right now, he had to make sure she lived to have a tomorrow. So he sat staring at the reports in front of him, wondering when he'd hit on something that triggered a clue, his mind drifting from the job at hand to the sounds of a woman making coffee in the kitchen.

Nice, domestic sounds. Homey and pleasant, peaceful and contented.

He could get used to that—having her in his home, in his life. He'd never before thought he would want that. He'd purposely stayed away from a lifetime commitment because of the nature of his work. That, and the shining example of living separately his parents had shown him made Shane a little gun-shy on matters of the heart.

His thoughts strayed ahead to kissing her and holding her and going on long rides through the hills with her.

He was so lost in that pleasant daydream, he forgot the reason he was sitting here.

Until he heard Katherine scream, followed by a crash in the kitchen.

EIGHT

Shane rushed into the kitchen with his weapon raised.

"Katherine?"

The kitchen was empty.

He'd protected many people in his lifetime. He'd been on security details in some of the roughest places on earth. But he'd never felt this kind of heart-shattering fear before, a fierce protective fear for the woman he was trying to guard. It tore through him, rendering him helpless. Until he remembered her beautiful smile.

"Katherine, answer me?"

"I'm here," she said, her voice barely above a whisper. "In the pantry."

He whirled toward the partially open door to the walk-in pantry just off the kitchen. Rushing toward that door, Shane yanked it open then pulled her into his arms. "What happened?"

Katherine clung to him for a minute then stepped back to wipe at her face. "I…I thought I saw someone in the window."

Shane pulled her behind him, switching off lights before he pivoted toward the long row of windows lining the kitchen. "Are you sure?"

She shook her head. "No, not really. I was standing by the sink and…the way the moonlight shot across the backyard…I thought I saw someone standing out there looking at me."

Shane absorbed that information then went into action. "Can you describe them?"

She took in a long breath then lifted her head toward him. "Shane, it looked like Jacob."

"Jacob? Your dead husband?"

"Yes," she said, putting her hands to her face. "That can't be possible. He's dead. I know he's dead. But it looked so much like him. That's why I screamed. I thought I was seeing a ghost."

Shane didn't believe in ghosts. "Listen to me," he said, holding her close again. "I have to go out and investigate."

"No!" She held him tight. "Don't go out there. They might kill you."

"Kit, I have to take a look." He lifted her away. "I want you to go to the back of the house and get Nina, okay? Stay there with her and Ricardo until I come back in."

"I'd rather go with you," she said, holding onto his shirt. "I need to see who that is out there."

"You can't. You'd only distract me. Let me walk around, see if they're still out there or if they left any tracks."

She looked doubtful, but she nodded her head, determination taking the place of her anxiety. "I'll give you ten minutes then I'm coming to find you, Shane." She stood back then turned toward the gun cabinet in the big den. "I know how to use several weapons."

Shane could tell she wouldn't back down so he

hurried her into the den and found a Smith & Wesson
.38 revolver. "Can you shoot this?"

She glanced at the gun then back at him. "Yes, I
can."

He handed her five copper-tipped bullets and then
whirled toward the door. "Go and find Nina and Ricardo. And don't use that unless you absolutely have no
other choice."

She nodded and took off down the hallway.

Her courage brought the beat back into Shane's heart.
He had a feeling Katherine was much stronger than
everyone around her realized. And that only added to
his growing fears and concerns for her.

Kit knocked on the sitting room door of Nina's apartment on the left wing of the big house and waited, the
warmth of the loaded revolver giving her strength.

Nina opened the door, took one look at the pistol then
pulled Kit into the room. "What's going on?"

"I thought I saw a prowler," Kit explained. "Shane
went to look, and he gave me this." She held the gun
down.

"I see," Nina said, motioning toward a floral couch.
"Come on in, Miss Katherine. You can wait here with
me."

"Where are your mother and Ricardo?"

"*Madre* is asleep in her room." Nina pointed toward
a small hallway. "And Ricardo is watching television in
his room."

"Let's check on them," Kit suggested, her gut instinct
telling her this wasn't over yet. She'd seen a human
standing outside that window. A man who looked

remarkably like Jacob—or at least someone who'd disguised himself as her late husband.

Nina gave her a worried look and led the way into the bedrooms. *Abuela* Silvia was fast asleep in her bed. Nina opened the door to Ricardo's room and gasped.

"He's not here!" She glanced around then pointed to his bed. "He left his cell phone here."

"Are you sure he was here?" Kit asked, dread coursing throughout her system.

"Yes." Nina went to the windows. "He's been known to sneak out during the night though. That boy is always wanting to be like Shane. Trying to protect us." She whirled to face Kit. "Do you think you saw *him* out the window?"

Kit didn't think Ricardo had purposely dressed up like Jacob to scare her. At least she hoped not. "No, no. This was a man, but it wasn't Ricardo. I screamed out when I saw him and he ran. Do you think Ricardo heard my screams and went outside?"

"He might have. I didn't hear anything," Nina said. "But I was listening to my iPod earlier. I barely heard your knock at the door." She looked around the empty room. "We need to find my son."

"Let's go," Kit said, wondering what they could do. Praying that Ricardo wouldn't get caught in the line of fire, or worse, she hurried with Nina toward the hallway leading back to the kitchen and garage. "We'll have to be careful. If someone is still out there, we could get hurt."

"Or Shane could mistake us for one of them," Nina said. Then she pulled out a cell phone. "I think we'd better call him and warn him that Ricardo isn't in his room."

"Good idea," Kit said as she slowly opened the heavy wooden door leading to the catwalk and the garage.

Nina listened then said, "Shane's not answering his phone. And I used the code we always use for alerts."

"That can't be good," Kit whispered. "Stay with me, Nina."

Nina held to the back of Kit's shirt, her lips moving in prayer as they crept along the hedges until they reached the corner of the big garage. "We can't go out there. Shane's not answering and that either means he's in trouble or he can't pick up. I have to make sure you're safe."

"I know," Kit replied. "But we have to do something. I can't leave him out there alone. And we have to find Ricardo, too. Let's stay together."

Nina clicked open her phone again. "Maybe I can send a text to Shane."

Kit waited while Nina punched at the keys, the sounds of the night putting her on edge. Every rustle, every gust of wind caused her skin to bristle. Where was Shane? Where was Ricardo? And who was doing this to her?

"No answer from him yet," Nina said, her tone full of apprehension. "I just hope wherever Shane is, he has my son with him. Ricardo knows not to leave when things are dangerous out there."

Kit interpreted that to mean whenever Shane was working on a case. Did he bring a lot of people here? She couldn't think about that right now. She just wanted to know he was safe and that Ricardo was okay, too. Holding the loaded gun down, she whispered to Nina. "You stay here. I'm going around to the front of the house."

"Are you sure?" Nina said, her breath rushed. "Shane won't be happy if I let something happen to you."

"I'll take full responsibility for my actions," Kit replied. "I can't stand around waiting."

She didn't have to wait. In the next seconds, they heard the pop of gunfire somewhere off in the distance.

Nina screamed and grabbed Kit. "We need to stay in the house."

But Kit was already running toward the garage. Hitting a button on the wall, she waited until the big doors opened. "I'm not going on foot. I'm taking my mother's bulletproof car." Grabbing the keys from the box on the wall, she turned back to Nina. "Get inside, get a gun and wait for me. I'm going to find Shane."

Shane glanced over at the boy holding the gun. "Ricardo, are you all right?"

"*Sì.*" Ricardo glanced over at Shane. "I messed things up, didn't I?"

Shane did a visual of the surrounding hills and trees, the buzz of his silenced cell telling him Nina was trying to locate him. But right now, they were penned in. He couldn't give Nina a signal until he got a handle on the situation. Praying that they were dealing with a lone intruder, he turned back to Ricardo.

"You didn't mess up," Shane said on a gush of a whisper. "You shouldn't have left the house, but now that you're here, we'll make the best of it. We've got him cornered and it's two to one. The odds are in our favor. Thanks for coming to help." Grabbing his cell, he texted a message to Nina.

"Sit tight. Ricardo OK. Keep Kit inside."

Ricardo's dark eyes flashed in the moonlight. "I had

to help. I heard her scream and then when I came around the corner, I saw him running."

Shane didn't know whether to send up a prayer of thanks for boys who sneaked out of the house behind their mothers' backs, or to give Ricardo a serious reprimand for leaving the house with a gun. "I'm glad you heard Kit and I'm glad you saw the prowler. But you'll have some explaining to do with your mother—about being out here with your gun on patrol. You went against my orders."

"I wanted to help," Ricardo replied. "And if I hadn't been out here, he might have gotten away."

"True," Shane replied, admiring the boy's fortitude. "Describe him to me again."

"He's tall with dark blond hair," Ricardo said. "And he has a gun."

"Yes, we can vouch for that based on the shots he just fired at us," Shane retorted, his sarcasm passing right by Ricardo's nervous energy. He'd also managed to get a brief look at the man. And Kit had been right; the man looked remarkably like her late husband based on the pictures Shane had seen of Jacob Atkins. Someone had gone to a lot of trouble to scare Katherine.

"What's the plan?" Ricardo asked, his rifle aimed toward the darkness in front of them.

Shane glanced around. They'd managed to hide behind an old bale of hay but the prowler was still out there. "We wait for a few minutes," he replied. "He'll make another move any minute now."

"How do you know that?"

"Because he has to get out of here before morning. And I can wait all night if I have to. If he's found here, he knows what will happen to him." Shane would take pleasure in questioning this impersonator.

Ricardo stared out into the night. "I'm so ready to learn, Shane. Why do I have to wait until after college?"

Shane and Ricardo had had this discussion before and now was not a very good time to go over the details again. But the boy needed to understand the commitment he was about to make. "Because you can't become a CHAIM agent until you're over twenty-one and you have your degree and good and proper training. You know the rules."

"I think the rules are *estúpido*," Ricardo said, his Hispanic heritage kicking in with each accented word. "I'm ready now."

"You're too young," Shane replied, remembering how he felt when he was a teenager. "It will come in due time." Then he leaned forward. "And right now, we need to focus on that shadow slinking across the pasture. That's not a longhorn. That's a human."

Ricardo looked through the scope of his rifle. "It's him. He's making a move just like you said. I can get a clean shot."

Shane held a hand against the boy's trigger finger. "Don't do anything, Ricardo. Do not shoot that gun. That's an order."

Ricardo frowned but he nodded and kept the gun trained on the shadowy figure moving through the grass and trees.

Shane lifted his own weapon, waiting for the right moment. He didn't want to kill the interloper, just hurt him enough to make him talk.

But before Shane could position himself to get in a

good shot, he heard a motor revving near the house. And then he looked up to see a sliver of bright yellow glowing in the moonlight as Sally Mae Barton's little sportscar zoomed past them.

"That was Miss Katherine," Ricardo said, his voice squeaky with shock. "What's she doing? Look, she's headed toward that man!"

"So I see," Shane replied, his nerves going into a jangling warning even while his phone hummed a message he didn't have to read.

Nina hadn't been able to keep Kit inside.

There was nothing more dangerous than a headstrong woman who was just a tad ticked off. Then he turned to Ricardo. "I need you to cover me. I have to get to that man before she does. Don't move from this spot and don't shoot to kill. Just rattle him a bit to keep him from hitting me or that car. It's supposed to be bulletproof, but I don't want to take any chances."

Ricardo nodded. "Is she gonna run him down?"

"Something like that, it appears," Shane said, gritting his teeth at the sound of gears shifting. This was not good. He should have never left the infuriating woman alone.

Kit was building up enough speed to flatten that intruder. That is, if the man didn't shoot her first.

NINE

She didn't want to do this.

Katherine had never deliberately tried to kill another human being but right now she didn't have any choice. Someone wanted to either scare her to death or make her come out of hiding.

"Congratulations," she said as she shifted gears. "You managed to do both."

Seeing the figure out in the pasture, she turned the little car around and headed straight toward where the surprised visitor was now hulking behind a lone cottonwood tree. What would Shane do in this situation? Maybe bump the man enough to knock the wind out of him? After all, if she mowed the man down and killed him, they might not get any answers. And she had to have answers. She was a logical, methodical person. She liked things in order. She needed answers and she needed to understand.

She watched the shadow up ahead, speeding along, building up steam with each shift of the gears when she saw another shadow out of the corner of her eye. Shane!

Then she heard gunshots. Worried that he'd been hit, she rammed the little car into Reverse and did a one-eighty toward Shane. Slamming on brakes, she opened the passenger door and shouted, "Get in!"

He was ready and waiting. Shane slid in and gave her a harried glance. "Fancy meeting you here."

"What now?" Kit asked, adrenaline making her hands shake. "I can still get to him."

Shane put a hand on hers over the gearshift. "Yes, I have no doubt you could do that. But Ricardo is out there, too. You don't want to run over Nina's only child, do you?"

Her heart clanked and rumbled like a rig pumping oil. "No, of course not. But we can't let him get away. I want to find out who he is and who sent him."

"Of course you do." Shane held her hand steady. "Ricardo has the man cornered behind those trees. And we're going to fall back on the old-fashioned way of getting to him."

"How?"

"We're going to rustle him up. Pretend he's a lost calf, so to speak. We circle back around and force him out of hiding. Can you do that, or do I need to drive?"

"I can do it," Kit said, relief replacing her need to hurt the man. She felt immensely better now that Shane was with her, but she was determined enough to take care of this culprit on her own if she had to. "I can do that."

Shane let go of her hand. "Okay then. Let's rodeo."

Kit didn't need any further instructions. She put the car into first and hit the gas, circling around the big moonlit pasture. "Where's Ricardo?"

"Behind that old bale of hay near the outbuilding to the west," Shane retorted. "He's holding off the intruder until he sees us coming over the north ridge."

"Got it." She maneuvered the purring car toward the copse of small trees and shrubs where the big cottonwood stood like a dark giant. "He went inside there."

"Yes, he's behind the cottonwood. He has nowhere else to hide."

"Okay. What do I need to do?"

Shane gave her an appreciative look then said, "Just head into the thicket. And watch for stumps or brush. We don't need to crash and we don't want to get shot. We just want to flush him out."

She stopped the car, revved the motor for a minute then hit first gear and plunged across the dry grass toward the bramble surrounding the cottonwood. "He's going to regret scaring me."

"I do believe he will at that," Shane replied. Then he put down the window on his side and leaned out, his gun pointed toward the trees.

It all happened in a matter of minutes, but in Shane's mind it seemed to drag on and on. Kit expertly drove the little car toward the cottonwood, bullets pelting all around them. She never blinked, she never wavered. In fact, he would always remember her face as being completely serene and completely determined, almost calm, as she "herded" the lone man hiding behind the tree out into the open.

Shane saw all of this in his mind even as he trained his weapon on the figure suddenly zigzagging in front of them. The man hurried away, the moonlight pinpointing him in the middle of the dipping terraces and hills.

And then, firing behind himself, the man practically ran right into the barrel of Ricardo's twelve-gauge shotgun. Ricardo, disobeying orders to stay hidden, pushed at the man with his gun, causing him to panic and drop his own weapon.

Kit centered the headlights on the two of them then slammed on the brakes. "We've got him."

"Yes, we do." Shane said a prayer and held his breath, hoping the boy wouldn't pull the trigger. Ricardo did not. He simply stood very still and held the gun trained on the man's chest.

And then he shouted, "Down on your knees."

The man, winded and tired and more than a little dazed, held up his gun and dropped it on the ground as he fell to his knees, all the while glancing behind him to make sure the little car didn't run him down.

Kit had stopped the sports car in a spray of dust and dirt just inches from the man's dark tennis shoes. Yanking her door open, she said, "Now we can find out why he's here."

Shane let out a deeply held breath. "Yes, I believe that will do, luv. Turn off the motor, please."

She looked reluctant, but she did as he asked. Then she got out of the car, her revolver held with both hands as she walked slowly toward the man.

Shane was right behind her, his own gun on the ready. Kit had done a marvelous job of staying cool under pressure but now the woman was at the boiling point. Shane prayed she'd stay calm and let him do the talking.

She looked so pristine, holding that gun like a true cowgirl ready for a shoot-out. Rather cute, if he didn't think about the circumstances.

Adorable. Kit Atkins was a brave, adorable, formidable woman who didn't back down.

Until she came face to face with the man in front

of her. Then she gasped and her hands went limp by her side. Shane caught the revolver before it hit the ground.

She couldn't believe what she was seeing.

"Jacob, is that you?"

The man grunted and held his head down.

Kit stepped forward, her hand reaching out into the night air. "Jacob, answer me, please?"

Shane moved between her and the man. "Sir, you're trespassing and you've given all of us quite a time tonight. You'd better start talking now, or things could get much worse for you."

The intruder finally looked up at them, his gaze shifting from Kit to Shane in a jittery dance. "I...I can't talk. They'll kill me."

Kit snapped out of her shock at the sound of his voice. "You're not my husband."

Then she let loose, grabbing the man by his black shirt, her fist hammering into his chest. "Tell me who you are, right now!"

Shane pulled her away then took over where she'd left off, lifting the man back to a standing position and fisting the man's shirt with his hands. "You'd better listen to her. She is not one to be trifled with. And while you're at it, take off that ridiculous disguise and tell us your name."

"Tim. Timothy Williams." The man slowly lifted the thick wig off his head to reveal dark, stringy hair. After dropping the wig to the ground, he tugged at the moustache over his lips. "Sorry, lady. They just told me to scare you and then to run."

"Well, you did," Kit said, sick to her stomach. "And

now I'm not scared, I'm angry. Is this some awful joke?"

"I don't know," the twitching man said. "They offered me a lot of money, told me how to get past security and…they told me to make sure you saw me and then to leave this somewhere." He held up a cell phone. "I was going to put it by the back door when you spotted me." He nodded toward Ricardo. "But when I saw him coming around the corner with a gun, I panicked and ran."

Shane took the cell phone the man pushed toward Kit. "Why a phone?"

Timothy shrugged and twitched some more. "I think they want to give you a message."

"So that's it?" Kit asked, thinking her life had turned into one of those weird crime scenes she'd see occasionally on the evening news. This man was either scared to death or needing his next fix, from the looks of him. "We just wait for a phone call." She turned to Shane. "What do you think?"

Shane looked over the disposal phone. "It looks like one of those cheap pay-as-you-go phones. Not traceable. But that could be a disguise, too. We'll just have to wait and see who calls us." He shot her a warning look. "In the meantime, Timothy and I need to have a little chat so we can get to know each other."

He yanked Timothy by the collar, bringing the kid nose to nose. "Come with me."

"Don't call the locals," Timothy hollered. "I'm on probation for distribution of illegal drugs. They'll send me back to prison."

Kit was right on his heels, anger fueling her need

for answers. "Well, you should have thought about that before you took this job."

The man shook his head then glanced up at her. "They offered me a lot of money, lady. I was gonna use it to get a new start." Then he shifted, his old boots stomping against the hard ground. "And they threatened me, said they'd make things look bad for me if I didn't cooperate."

Kit stepped so close to the man, Shane feared she was about to wring his scrawny neck. "Well, you can double that for me. If you don't tell us everything you know, I will make you pay in every way imaginable. I can promise you that."

Shane noted how little Timmy cowered underneath that feminine declaration. "I'm sorry, lady, okay?"

"Don't worry, luv," Shane said to Kit as he pushed the man toward the house, Ricardo helping him to guard the culprit. "We'll have some answers before sunrise, I can promise you that."

"Good," she said. "And I hope whoever gave him that phone will call soon. I'd really like to talk to them, too."

"Just be patient," Shane said. "Do you feel up to driving the car back to the house?"

Kit nodded. "I'll be fine. Unless I decide to finish him off right here and now."

"Now, darlin', take a deep breath and drive the car back slowly, very slowly so I can keep an eye on you while I walk Timothy home," Shane said, his gaze moving over the jumpy man in front of him. "I think our friend Tim here has had enough excitement for one night."

"Don't let her behind that wheel again," Timothy said, glancing over his shoulder. "She's crazy."

"Not crazy," Shane said, pushing hard on the man's backbone for emphasis. "Just really, really mad that you played such a despicable trick on her. And she won't forget it, not for a long time." He glanced over at Kit, his eyes holding hers in a plea. "That's why she needs a quiet drive—to calm her nerves." He motioned toward Ricardo. "Ride with her, will you?"

Timothy looked sick to his stomach. And Shane feared that underneath her anger, Kit was very close to the same.

Two hours later, Timothy Williams still wouldn't tell them anything other than some "rich-looking stranger" approached him in a bar about twenty miles up the road and asked him if he'd like to make some spending money.

"I said sure," Timothy told them, his beady eyes full of woe each time he glanced up at Shane in the big, shadowy office at the back of the house. "He took me to this hotel room and showed me the file he had on me. That dude knew everything about me, good and bad. He offered me ten thousand dollars and told me if I didn't do exactly as he said, he'd get me thrown back into prison on some trumped-up charge. Said he'd make sure they found drugs in my apartment."

"What else can you tell us?" Shane asked, his patience wearing very thin.

"That's it, man," Timothy insisted. "He gave me the instructions. Put on the wig and mustache and go to this place out in the middle of nowhere. Gave me the exact location but I got lost anyway. Told me to find the woman, scare her then leave the phone by the back door where you'd be sure to find it. Never seen a place so hard to find, especially the way he had me come in on the other side of the river. Just got lucky, seeing her at the kitchen window. I was gonna drop the phone and get out of here."

"Describe this man to me one more time," Shane said, glancing over at where Kit sat nursing a cup of strong coffee. She was quiet, too quiet. And she looked exhausted, her usually vivid green eyes slanting down in a forest-like darkness.

"I told you, man. He was tall with reddish-brown hair cut close to his head. He wore a fancy suit and didn't even break a sweat, even when he was telling me exactly what might happen to me if I messed up." He shrugged, bent his head down. "And now, I've done that. I was supposed to report back to him—"

He stopped, his Adam's apple bobbing as he lowered his eyes, his gaze shuttered again.

Shane grabbed him, yanking him up and out of the chair. "Where and when?"

Timothy shook his head. "No, man. I can't tell you. He'll kill me."

"And I'll kill you if you don't," Shane said, his deadly tone full of a calm intent. He'd had enough for one night.

Timothy's fear palpitated throughout his skinny frame, causing him to tremble. "I can't do that. He's dangerous. He made it clear what would happen to me—"

"Perhaps *I* haven't made *myself* clear then," Shane said, his hand still on Timothy's torn, dirty shirt. "I can do just as much damage to your good name, my friend. And I can make things much worse than your mysterious employer ever promised you." He leaned close, so close he could smell the fear radiating off Timothy's scrawny body. "I know this place, far away, where we send people who don't cooperate with us. You'd disappear, Timmy. You'd cease existing all together. You won't die but you'll certainly wish you could." He stood back, his gaze moving from Timothy to Katherine, hoping she'd believe his exaggerated threats. "You don't realize what you've done or with whom you're dealing. This woman's father will come after you and make you suffer, just as she told you earlier."

Katherine sat there, her eyes centered on Timothy Williams, her expression bordering on murderous. But she didn't threaten the man and she didn't speak up as Shane had expected, which scared him more than he was willing to admit. What was she thinking? What was she planning?

Deciding he'd talk to her later, he looked down at Timothy. "I'm going to give you one more chance to tell me the truth, Mr. Williams. If you aren't completely honest with me, things are going to go from bad to worse for you in a very short time."

Timothy looked up at Shane, terror in his dark eyes. "He said—"

The disposable phone lying on Shane's desk rang.

And before Shane could grab it and take the call, Katherine had it up to her ear, every muscle in her face strained and tense as she spoke into the receiver.

So that was what she'd been waiting for.

"Hello?" she said, her tone full of tremors.

Shane held his breath as he watched her face go pale.

TEN

Kit gripped the phone so hard her knuckle bones protested. "Trudy?"

"It's me, suga'," Trudy said, her voice sounding faraway and strained.

Kit couldn't tell if her friend was laughing or crying. "Are you all right?"

"I've been better," Trudy said. "How about you?"

"I'm fine," Kit said, her gaze locking with Shane's. "Trudy, why are you calling me on this phone?"

Trudy let out a long, shuddering sob. "No one would let me talk to you. You're not answering your phone. I've left messages with your staff at your office and at home. Your daddy wouldn't even talk to me."

"They were all told not to take any calls," Katherine explained, her mind whirling with fear and concern. "I'm all right. But how did you get this phone number?"

"They gave it to me," Trudy replied. "Told me I had to talk to you, make you understand."

Kit motioned to Shane. "Understand what?"

Shane dumped Timothy Williams in the chair and whispered, "Don't make a move or you'll die right here." Then he hurried around the desk to Katherine. "What's going on?"

She mouthed, "I don't know." Then turning her attention back to Trudy, she said, "Trudy, tell me what's wrong. Tell me why you're involved in this."

"They…they have me, Kit," Trudy said. "They took me right out of my bed a few hours after the attack at the gala. They're upset that you didn't die that night so now they want you to come to them. Just to talk."

"They? Who? Talk about what?"

"I don't know—something to do with Mexico, I think. I don't even know where I am. It's dark and they only come in to bring me food. I'm in some big house or some sort of building. I know that from all the stairs I had to go up to get to this room. I—"

Trudy stopped talking then Kit heard a quick noise that sounded like a pop. "Trudy? Are you there?"

"I'm here," Trudy replied, her voice weaker now. "Sorry about that. I said too much. My keeper had to remind me to stick to the script."

Katherine's heart pumped so hard it hurt to breathe. "What do you mean?"

"Kit, I've been kidnapped. They're trying to get to you through me. They want you to come out of hiding and talk to them or…well…they're threatening to kill me. But I'm not scared of these bullies."

Katherine heard another whacking sound, followed by a moan. "Trudy?"

It took a few seconds before Trudy responded. "That's all I can say, except—don't do it. They know where you are, so get out of there and don't come near these people. We'll talk later. Gotta go."

Kit heard Trudy's high-pitched scream then the connection was lost. Staring down at the ugly black phone, she put her hand to her mouth. "They have Trudy.

Somebody kidnapped her and they're holding her. I think they've been beating her. Shane?"

He pulled her into his arms, his hand resting on her hair. "What else did she say?"

Katherine glanced over his shoulder at Timothy. "She said they want me to come out of hiding and talk to them." Her panicked gaze held his. "Something about Mexico."

Why did Mexico keep popping up on the radar?

Shane pulled back to stare down at her. "Or?"

She wiped at her eyes. "They'll kill Trudy if I don't do it. She said they were angry that they didn't kill me the other night and now they're threatening her unless I come to them and talk. She told me not to do what they wanted, but I have to. We have to help her."

She hit keys on the phone. "There's a number. I have to call it back."

"No, don't. They'll have it blocked," Shane said, taking the phone from her. "I'll have to analyze it more and try to do a reverse trace. But without the number that might be impossible. But if you call them back, they can verify Trudy was talking to you. They'll keep her alive. She's the link to you."

Kit couldn't live with that. The thought of Trudy being held and tortured made her dizzy with nausea. "So we just wait?"

"It's okay," Shane said, his eyes a calculating blue. "First things first, luv." He pointed to the man in the chair. "We get this one to tell us where he was supposed to meet up with his friend and then we go from there. Maybe we can track them back to Trudy."

Katherine pulled away to stare up at him. "It might

be too late by then. We don't have time. They obviously know I'm here with you since they sent him here."

"Yes, but maybe they sent him to *make sure* you were here," Shane said. "Why send him just to scare you and bring you a phone? They sent an assassin to kill you the other night. Why didn't they come in and try to take you?"

"No one could reach me," she tried to explain. "My father wouldn't take Trudy's calls. They must have grabbed her immediately after the attack, hoping she'd be able to talk to me or get to me. And now they know I'm here but they're afraid to show their faces." She shot another boiling look at the man in the chair. "So they sent him instead to do their dirty work."

Shane glared at Timothy Williams then turned back to Kit. "We're monitoring all incoming calls to your father's location, so we might be able to pinpoint something there. Any wrong word could put you in even more danger now that they've verified you're here."

"So you'll cut me off from my best friend, let her suffer just to protect me. I won't do that. I can't."

She saw his expression change. It was so quick she almost missed it, but Katherine saw the cautious way he went blank, saw the look of doubt in his eyes.

A sick feeling pooled inside her stomach, making her feel queasy. "You don't still think Trudy had something to do with all of this?"

"I can't rule out anyone, Kit. And now it looks as if she's right in the thick of things. Someone found out I brought you here."

"But it couldn't have been Trudy. She didn't know where you were taking me that night."

"But your parents trust her. They might have inadvertently said something to tip her off. She might have caved and given out a clue. Maybe that's why our friend here showed up tonight. Someone knew how to get to you."

"But she said my parents weren't taking her calls. How could they tell her anything when *they* didn't even know where you were taking me?"

"True, that doesn't make sense but neither does the fact that they tried to kill you and now they just want to talk to you. Someone figured out where you are. Somehow. They might have managed to get a tracker on your mother's car before we even arrived at Eagle Rock. She did say she takes that car out a lot."

Frantic, Kit shook her head. "We can worry about that later. Shane, if they're trying to force information out of Trudy, we need to find her right now!"

Pulling away, she pushed past Shane and lunged for Timothy Williams. Grabbing him by the arm, she said, "You'd better tell me where you're supposed to meet this man, do you understand? They have my best friend and they'll kill her. Tell me now, do you hear me?"

Shane managed to pull her off before she could claw the man's eyes out, but that didn't stop Katherine from taking action. Lifting away from Shane, she said, "I'm okay. I'm fine. Just get some answers out of him." Giving the man one last scalding look, she turned back to Shane. "Make him talk. I can't stand to be in the same room with him anymore."

Then, the black phone tucked in one fisted hand, she turned and left the room, intent on taking her mother's car and going back to Austin. They wanted her to come to them? Well, then, that's what she'd do.

And she prayed she'd get there in time to save Trudy.

Shane's gut was burning with all the fire of a tree hit by lightning.

Ulcers. That's what he had to show for with this job.

And now was not a good time for ulcers to flare up. He had a bad feeling that Kit wasn't going upstairs to retire for the night. And he had a bad feeling that Timothy Williams wasn't going to give up the goods without a fight.

But the worst of his feelings kept coming back to Mexico. What was going on there? And did this attack have anything to do with Kit's upcoming trip? Mexico was full of dangerous drug cartels and corrupt people in authority. What had Katherine gotten herself caught up in?

Which crisis to handle first?

Turning to Timothy, Shane decided he'd deal with him after he kept Katherine from doing something foolish. He needed to get that phone from her.

"Okay, my friend. I need to take care of some business. So I want you to sit tight, as they say here in America, and wait for me."

He buzzed Nina and told her to bring rope and a gun. Then he stared down at the shivering man in the chair. "Someone will be in shortly to watch you. And while you're sitting here, think really long and hard about your options. Your mysterious benefactor isn't here to protect you and as I said before, I can make you disappear. You'll have to decide which way you want to handle this."

Timothy turned a sickly white-pale. "Man, don't do this. Don't hold me here. He's waiting for me."

Shane leaned close. "He wants her to come out of hiding. We know that now because they're holding her friend and they forced her to make the call. You did complete your mission but now because you failed to report back you've become expendable. He sent you here so he could stay in hiding and protect his identity. Your identity doesn't matter anymore. Do you actually think he'll let you live now?"

"You don't get it, do you?" Timothy shouted. "He's gonna kill her, too. He sent me instead of coming here himself because he wants to talk to her first but he can't reveal his face. The man who hired me isn't the main man. He was just the hired help, like me. But the big shot behind all of this wants to flush her out—and you, too. She has something they need."

Shane leaned down, a hand on each of the chair arms. "Go on."

Timothy held up his hands, palms out. "I don't know what it is. Nobody's bothered to share that with me and they told me not to use that phone for anything—just make sure she got it. They gave me the wig and mustache and showed me this picture of her dead husband. Said to make it look good to shake her up. They knew you'd come running and find the phone. But I messed up and now I need to get back to the meeting point and explain."

"Oh, you won't have an opportunity to explain. They are going to kill you and leave you at my doorstep."

Timothy's expression turned petulant. Then he made a plea. "If I help you, can you help me?"

Shane let out a derisive chuckle. "There is no help for any of us, Timothy. We're all in a fine mess here."

Timothy was sweating now, grasping for tidbits of information as reality set in and his last fix wore off. "Look, whatever it is he's got on your woman, he thinks it's worth killing her—after he finds it. He needs to get her to talk, but after that things look bad. That's all I know, I swear."

His words sent a chill rushing down Shane's backbone.

"You need to tell me where you were supposed to meet him, do you understand?"

Timothy shook his head. "I can't be sure. I don't know except he was going to pick me up out on the same road where he dropped me—that old stagecoach road that runs in front of your property—that long dirt lane. Said he'd pick me up around dawn and then he'd pay me the rest of my money and drop me off at the bus station. That's it, honest. I just want to go to the road and wait."

Shane's burning gut told him differently. Timmy might be lying to protect himself from a very dangerous man. Shane could become dangerous, could end this right now. He had to find Katherine, but he also needed someone to knock some sense into this idiot's head. And he wouldn't put Nina and her family at risk by asking them to do it.

"I need backup," he said to himself. They were no longer safe here. Then he looked over at Timmy. "I hate to do this, but I'm going to have to call in someone I can trust to watch out for you and…persuade you to remember more. You won't be meeting up with anyone out on the road at sunup. But I will. And if you're lying to me, my friend will take care of you, one way or another." And his friend could offer protection while Shane planned their next move.

Tim glared at him, his eyes wide with fear. "You're making a big mistake."

"We'll see." Shane dialed a number he hadn't used in a long time and prayed his fellow teammate would be there. It rang several times then he heard a loud, snarling grunt.

"This better be good."

The voice rasped over the wire, making Shane wonder if he'd chosen wisely. Top command would tell him to leave the Warrior out of this. Too much, too soon.

Well, the top command wasn't here. "Paco, is that you, my friend?"

"Who wants to know?"

"Now don't be coy," Shane said, hoping Luke "Paco" Martinez would be in a good frame of mind. "I need help and I need it rather quickly. How soon can you be in Texas?"

Another grunt then a sigh. "Tell me some Scripture."

Shane smiled in spite of the fire pit in his belly and recited the last verse of Job, Chapter 21, hoping Paco would pick up the code for his location at the remote ranch. "The counsel of the wicked is far from me."

"How soon do you need me, brother?"

"Yesterday," Shane said, breathing a sigh of relief. "I have a man here who can't seem to remember who sent him to terrorize our client. Think you could help him recall?"

"I'm on my way."

And that was all the confirmation he needed from the Warrior. If anyone could make Timmy give up the goods, it would be Paco Martinez. The man had ice water running through his veins and he wasn't the sociable, small-talk type. Paco liked to get down to business right away.

"You're in for a real treat," Shane told Timmy. "I picked the best of the best to come and sit with you—a war hero who misses the fight, so to speak. But until my friend arrives, I'll have my staff bring you some breakfast. And they'll be watching you until your keeper gets here."

After a knock at the door, he got up, grabbed his gun and turned to stare down at Williams. He let Nina and Ricardo in, watching as Ricardo set a plate of food down then securely tied Timmy's hands. "Nina will feed you. Don't try anything stupid." He nodded to Ricardo. The boy leveled his infamous shotgun on the prisoner. "Oh, and Timmy, they both know how to use every weapon we have in this place. Don't tease them now, you understand?"

He left with the sound of Timmy's whining demands echoing inside his head. Shane didn't have time to worry about Timmy's comfort, however.

He had to get to Katherine before she bolted and went out to fix this mess on her own.

The phone had rung again. "Trudy? Trudy, is that you?"

Someone had been there, listening. But they didn't say a word. Then the connection had ended once again.

Kit looked down the long hallway, the dark shards

of a cloudy night streaming through the many windows to remind her she didn't have much time. She had to get out of here before Shane tried to stop her.

Her overnight bag in her hand, she made her way down the stairs, her sneakers barely brushing against the polished wood of the steps. Glancing around the back hallway, she knew Silvia was still asleep. And Nina and Ricardo were probably in the kitchen having a heart to heart about the boy's bold and courageous acts last night.

Wishing she could thank Ricardo again for helping them capture Timothy Williams, Kit kept her eyes straight ahead. She only had to make it to the back door leading to the garage and her mother's car.

No one was in the back hallway, so she carefully opened the door and looked out into the murky shadows. The clouds parted to show an angry crescent moon lifting across the foothills, hovering over the trees like a sinister smile.

Such a beautiful night in spite of the fitful clouds. Nothing about it indicated that she'd had to chase a crazy man all over the big, sloping pasture or that they could have all been killed if that man's misguided bullets had hit any of them.

Thankful that Shane's office was secluded toward the back of the house, she opened the smaller back garage door then the big one that enclosed the garage from the other side, using the code she'd learned from watching Shane and Nina.

Then she was inside, the bright yellow car waiting like a beacon to help her make her escape. Taking a long, calming breath, she inhaled in relief and clicked on the remote key pad to unlock the little car.

And felt that now-familiar hand reaching out to touch hers. Kit turned to find Shane staring down at her, his eyes as rich and full of clouds as the conflicted late night sky.

"Going somewhere, Katherine?"

ELEVEN

Shane could see the stubborn all over her face.

"I'm going home," she said, pulling her hand away. "I have to help Trudy."

"We're going to help Trudy," he said, blocking her way into the car. "But not like this. You can't walk into their trap, Katherine. They know you're here now."

"Oh, and what am I supposed to do then? Just sit around here waiting for them to come after me again? If this has something to do with my trip to Mexico maybe I can talk to them and make sense of this."

"These are not sensible people, Katherine. I can still protect you here."

"I wasn't protected last night. That man walked right up to the kitchen window."

Shane couldn't find a retort for that. She was right. In spite of all his security measures, someone had breached the perimeters of his property. "I'm sorry," he said, hoping she'd be reasonable. "I plan to rectify that. I've called in reinforcements."

She shook her head, causing her shimmering hair to fall around her face. "You can bring an army here and it won't matter. I can't stay here, knowing they have my best friend, knowing they took her to get to me. Can't you understand that?" She waited but apparently didn't like his silence. "Oh, right. You actually suspect she might somehow be involved in all of this."

"She could be," he said, wondering how much he should tell her in order to keep her here. Her friend Trudy had married into old Texas money and since her husband's death she'd made some questionable investments, dealing with some unsavory people. He couldn't put his finger on it yet, but something didn't sit well with all of Trudy's after-hours soirees. And the fact that Trudy had been the one on the other end of that phone line. Shane didn't know what was nagging at him, some memory, something he'd processed that refused to come to the surface. But each time he thought of Trudy Pearson, his gut started burning.

Katherine fumed a response. "Do you have proof of anything? Do you know things about the woman *I've* known since grade school?"

"I told you, we're investigating every possible avenue."

"Right and that's supposed to make me feel better about them holding her and slapping her around? I don't think so. If you don't let me go right now, Shane, I'll find another way. If I have to bust Timothy loose to help me, I'll do it. You can't hold me here against my will."

Shane knew when he'd been bested. She'd gone from ladylike charm to getting down and dirty. He opted to change the subject. "Do you still have the phone?"

She watched his face, probably looking for signs of weakness or treachery. "I do. They wanted me to have it, so now it's mine. And you're not going to take it from me."

"I wasn't planning on taking it from you," he said,

grabbing her bag. "But I do need to analyze it and try to locate where it was purchased. I might be able to figure things out if I can trace the serial number."

"I don't have time for you to do that. And I need it in case they call me back."

Shane considered that. It would be nearly impossible to trace a disposable phone but he could at least try. But they'd probably send her another message soon. He'd want to listen in on that. First, he had to take care of the beautiful woman trying to get away from him. "Let's go then."

Her shock was priceless. "Go where?"

"You want to leave, then we leave. I promised your father I wouldn't let you out of my sight and I promised your mother I'd take care of you. That means if you leave then I go with you. Besides, they know you're here now. They might send their own reinforcements if you don't do as they ask."

He tried to look relaxed, as if they were about to go on a weekend trip. Then he glanced toward the skies. "I'd hoped to ride out to the road on horseback at dawn to see if I could track anyone else. Timmy said a man was supposed to pick him up at dawn out just off the main road. I have every reason to doubt him but I'd like to test that theory at least. If we could get to that person, we'd have a connection that might quickly lead us to Trudy."

Wariness settled in her green eyes, making them go dark. "Okay, I have to admit I wondered why they didn't just come here and try to take me. Why all the games?"

Shane debated whether to tell her everything. Maybe putting the hard facts out there would stop her.

"They obviously want you alive now, darling. Very much alive. They've located you and now they've verified that through the phone. They want to make you come to them so they won't blow their cover after the gala fiasco. But I can't let you go out there all on your own to face them. Once they get what they want from you, they'll kill you. And if you can't give them what they want because you don't have anything or you don't know anything, they will certainly kill you anyway. I have no doubt of that."

"Just like they'll kill Trudy if I don't help her."

"She's safe for now. She's their bargaining chip." He touched a hand to her cheek. "If you can give me a few hours, we could take some horses and ride out to watch the road. That way, I'd know you're safe and we could wait for the next call. And I assure you there will be a next call."

"Why wouldn't you set up a trace somehow?"

"A trace won't work on this type of cheap, pay-as-you-go phone. These people know what they're doing and they probably bought several phones at once. Next time they call you, they'll just switch to a different one, with a different return number. Then they'll throw them away as they go so we can't trace them."

"They've already called again," she said, guilt coloring her expression.

"Why didn't you tell me that right away? What did they say?'

She looked down, her shoulders shifting. "Nothing. I asked for Trudy and I heard someone there, but they wouldn't respond."

"Then you verified to them that you truly were the person Trudy spoke to the first time. That's what they needed to know for now. And I'm sure they have an elaborate system in place to respond to you without being detected. They'll kill Timmy, not help him get away. That's why I need to get up to the main road and meet whoever was coming for him. That's the next link in the chain. And that will better serve us than you rushing off without any forethought to find your friend."

She glanced at the car, longing and aggravation centered in her eyes. "What if it's too late? What if they'd already killed her now that they've located me?"

Shane put his hands on her shoulders. "I've called in people to help, luv. My fellow team member Paco Martinez is on his way here to take over with Timmy's care and feeding. We can only hold him for so long before we have to turn him over to the authorities. And I've alerted your father to the situation with your friend. He's putting men on it right now. Don't you think that makes more sense than trying to take off on your own? And don't you know me well enough to realize I would do anything in my power to help another human, especially a defenseless woman who might be in danger?"

She stared up at him, her eyes turning a forest green, all misty and lush. Then she reached up and wrapped her arms around his neck. "I have to learn to trust you."

Shane was so astonished at her words and so aware of her there in his arms, he had to search hard for his next breath. "And I have to remember to tell you everything right up front from now on." He pulled her close, his words touching on her sweet-smelling hair. "Especially if I get this kind of reaction."

Realizing she was still holding him, she stood back into a less intimate stance, proper decorum back in full force. "Ready?"

She'd managed to surprise him yet again. "Uh, I think. With you, luv, I'm pretty much ready for anything. But apparently, never quite prepared."

She gave him a stern look. "Now that I know someone cares about Trudy, I can take care of the rest. Let's go on that horseback ride out to the road."

"Are you sure?"

She looked doubtful for a second but she lifted that defiant chin and put on her best showtime face. "Yes." She dropped the phone into the pocket of her jeans.

"Right, then." He took her bag and put it on a nearby shelf. "I'll alert Nina and then we'll go get prepared to saddle up."

"And what about the man you left chained to a chair in your office?"

"Ricardo and Nina are entertaining our guest for now. I told you I called in help. I've asked a highly qualified team member to come here and take care of that little bit of trouble. And to handle any other surprise guests who might follow. So that leaves us to go about our business."

"And what will this highly qualified team member do?"

He guided her toward the path just past the garage leading to the stables. "You don't need to worry about that."

"Oh, I see. You think I can't handle it. What happened to being upfront with me about everything?"

"I'd rather not give you the details on that particular subject." Rapping his fingers against his jeans, he said, "Look, Paco has his own methods for getting information out of people. The man is an uncelebrated war hero and he's a bit rough around the edges. He can be scary to some."

"I don't scare easily."

"I can clearly see that."

"Can you? Can you really see me, Shane?"

She studied him, her cool green eyes assessing him with a clarity that left Shane feeling stripped of all the facades he so carefully used. For once in his life, he wanted to let go of the secrecy and the facades and take her into his arms and kiss her silly. But he didn't do that.

Not yet.

He did, however, adhere to the new "up-front" rule. "Oh, yes, my dear, I see you very clearly. And you take my breath away."

Her smile wasn't quite happy. "Always the debonair charmer. I just hope you didn't charm me into making the wrong decision about this."

"I'm telling the truth," he replied, his fear of how she made him feel topping any tactics Paco could bring. Or the fact that she'd figured him out so completely.

"I'll have to take your word on that," she said as she purposely strolled into the stable. "Let's go track a bad man."

Shane sent up a prayer of thanks then punched some numbers into his phone. "Mr. Barton, sir. I'm still with Katherine, but we had a breach of security. The Warrior is on his way. And I've convinced Katherine we need to remain at this location for now. I'll give you a full update later. Katherine is secure, but she's had word from Trudy. Once we finish clearing up a few matters, we'll relocate to another safe house, and I'll explain more thoroughly."

That caused Katherine to wrinkle her lovely brow and frown at him. And caused her father to launch into a tirade that wasn't nearly so lovely.

"Warwick, I thought I could trust you on this. How in the world? This is dangerous. Too dangerous. I don't like you taking her all over the infernal country. It's risky, especially with Trudy missing, too. Where is she?"

"All we know is that she's safe for now. Have you been able to find out anything on her, sir?"

"Nope, and I've got several men on it. It's as if the woman has disappeared off the face of the earth. You let me know the minute you hear from her again. I'll keep you posted if I hear from her."

Shane decided not to share any more information with Katherine's father. It would only worry her even more. "Yes, sir. And I'll keep Katherine safe until we can decide our next move." Gerald Barton didn't need the details, and Shane couldn't explain Trudy's strange behaviour.

"I'll give you one more chance, Warwick, and if that doesn't work, you'd better bring my daughter home. This hiding out in the hills is just too dangerous. Where are you, anyway?"

He held the phone away, letting Katherine's father shout himself out. "Yes, sir, I realize that. It's dangerous but your daughter wanted to leave by herself to go and find her friend. She's very worried. I've convinced her to let others handle that matter. I won't let any harm come to her but it's too risky to leave our location right now. And I'd rather not say where that is."

Gerald Barton let out a loud grunt. "Just like her mama, always taking matters into her own hands. I tell you, I didn't like it when my wife snuck y'all out of here and I don't like it now. Not one bit."

Shane listened, heard a long sigh then Gerald said, "So what's your plan, anyway?"

"I'll get back to you on that, sir." He glanced over at Katherine, spoke reassuring words into the phone again then ended the call, not quite sure about the plan at all. Or if he'd have a job or not whenever this was over. "Your father sends his best, luv."

Katherine sent him a slight nod then walked to a gorgeous mare named Peaches and began saddling her with expert precision.

Watching her, Shane called the house and explained the situation to Nina. "Paco Martinez is flying in from Arizona. His code name is the Warrior. He should be here by mid-morning to take custody of our visitor. He has full access to security measures, understand? You can trust Paco with your life so do whatever he tells you to do. And he'll keep young Ricardo under his wing, too." Then he told her he'd be out of range for a couple of hours and explained that Katherine would be with him.

Shane dropped the sleek phone into his pocket. "Well now that I've reassured everyone that you're safe and I have things under control, we have a couple of hours before we're off to see if we can find our pickup man. We'll take the long way around."

By the time they made it to the main road, taking the path that meandered through the stream to avoid leaving too many tracks, the sun was giving a valiant try of coming over the distant foothills. But the low dark clouds surrounding it didn't bode well.

"We might have missed him," Shane said, his gray stallion Hercules snorting in the bluish-pink dawn. "We'll leave the horses here, though, and walk the rest of the way."

"Why didn't you just drive us up here?" she asked, her tone low.

"In that shouting yellow car? I think not."

"You have other vehicles made for off-road. We're out in the open now."

He couldn't argue that point. "I was afraid you'd take off in a car or a Rhino or a four-wheeler for that matter. Or run yet another criminal down."

"I might have done all of that."

"This way, we have a getaway plan and we can hide in places a vehicle can't get into."

She nodded at that. "Makes sense in a cowboy kind of way."

He motioned to her to follow him into some thick bramble by the back entrance, a few miles from the main gate. "This is the way our Timmy entered. He left enough evidence to spook a bull." He pointed to some cut fence markings and footprints. "See that broken bramble. He must have come through right through over there."

She eyed the trampled leaves and torn branches. "I thought this place was solid and secure."

Shane glanced around, making sure they were alone. "I don't have heavy security on the backside of the property because this is rough country—overgrown with trees and bramble, full of snakes, the occasional bear, coyotes, and not many markers. Easy to get lost. Only a fool would venture through here."

"Well, that just about describes him."

Shane put a finger to his lips. "Let's go settle down by the fence." Then he stopped and tugged her close. "I only brought you with me to keep an eye on you. Don't do anything—just watch and wait."

She gave him a long, hard stare. "I'll try."

"I mean it, Katherine. If something should happen to me, you run as fast as your pretty legs can carry you back to Peaches and Hercules. And you get on that mare and ride for home. Hercules will know to follow—or lead if need be. Do you understand?"

"Got it. Ride for home."

Shane's stomach sizzled and singed. He popped an antacid tablet. "Did you pack that revolver?"

"Of course I did," she said. Then she pulled the gun out from the back of her sweater. "Just in case."

Shane was afraid to think about what she might do. "Don't use that gun, Katherine." Then he changed that to "Use it to protect yourself if you must."

"Don't worry about me," she said. "Let's just get this man."

They crept through the bramble, hiding behind shrubs and bushes until they were near the gap in the heavy wire fence. Shane patted a spot underneath an aged elm tree, making sure no unwelcome creatures waited for them. "Sit."

Katherine sat down beside him then looked up at the sky. "Shane, I think it's going to—"

Rain.

The first fat drops hit them, sending a chilling wetness down Shane's back. He scooted her closer to the trunk of the tree, hoping the thick branches would serve as protection. "Great. Just great."

Then the sky opened up into a real downpour. He put his arm around Katherine, pulling her close. "Sorry."

She looked up at him, her gaze locking with his just as a big clap of thunder rattled behind them. Shane saw the lightning crashing across the sky then heard another round of thunder, but that couldn't match the pounding inside his ears.

Katherine must have felt it, too, this roaring of awareness and attraction. She leaned close, a sigh escaping her parted lips. Shane held her, saw the acceptance in her eyes, took that same acceptance into his heart. There would be no turning back now. None at all. But for once, he didn't want to turn back.

And that's when he gave in and leaned over to kiss her.

But that was also when they heard a motor revving just around the curve in the road.

A big vehicle was headed toward them.

TWELVE

Shane pushed Kit down, the sound of thunder above them warring with the engine of the big truck moving slowly up the muddy dirt lane. His pulse had quickened for another reason. It was showtime.

"We have company, darling," he said, his heart still recovering from kissing her. "Stay down."

She looked up at him, her expression full of surprise, but he couldn't be sure if that surprise stemmed from the situation or the fact that he'd broken all protocol and fallen for her. They'd deal with that later.

The rain would give them a measure of cover, he thought as he crouched behind the big elm tree, lush shoots sprouting around him near its wrinkled trunk. And the tree would act as a cover of sorts. "Let's get a look."

"Be careful," Kit said behind him, her words as strong and sure as her kiss had been just a minute ago.

He carried that thought with him as he crept to the fence line and squinted into the storm. "One. A lone driver. That's good for us." Studying the surrounding woods, Shane prayed no one else had come along for the ride. "And from the description Timmy gave me, it looks like our man."

He had to stop that lone driver and keep him alive to give them information, so he pulled out the pistol he'd brought along for this purpose, covering it with the tail of his damp shirt.

"What are you going to do?" Kit asked, her hand on his back as she crouched beside him.

"I'm going to blow out both of the front tires of that truck then I'm going to grab the driver."

"Oh, all right. Good luck with that."

He glanced over his shoulder at her. "And you have a better plan?"

"Let me act as decoy. If he sees me here, he'll think he has what he came for."

"No. Absolutely not. I won't put you at risk."

"I won't be at risk. You said they want me alive. He wouldn't dare do anything to me."

The lady had a point. But so much could go wrong. "Not a good idea, luv."

"What if I just poke my head out and he spots me? I'll hide and then you can take over from there. I'll cover you—I have my own gun, remember?" She waited a delicate beat then added, "Shane, we're running out of time."

Shane didn't like this. But he figured she'd jump up and follow him out onto the road if he didn't involve her in the plan. Katherine Atkins liked to be involved in things. This much he knew.

The rain stopped as quickly as it had started, but the sky didn't look finished. The storm would move back in. He needed to end this now.

"All right," he said on a winded hiss as the truck came closer. "Just stand up and wave. Then duck down and don't move until you see me again."

"Yes, sir." She pushed at her hair, ever the glamour girl. "I'll only be a minute."

Shane's heart stopped beating for that tiny minute. He watched her, watched the truck, watched the driver, and motioned to her. "I'm going through the fence. Stay here."

Kit played it to the hilt, lifting up, the wind and rain pushing at her glistening wet curls. Then she waved both hands in the air in a motion that immediately got the driver's attention. The big truck slid to a grinding halt and the driver stepped out.

And right into Shane's gun aimed at the back of his head.

Kit sank down in the bushes, her gun trained on the driver as Shane pushed the man back toward the truck and began questioning him. "Who's with you?"

"No one." The well-dressed red-haired man held up his hands. "I got lost out here. Got off the main road and wound up here. What's this all about, Mister?"

"Don't lie to me," Shane said, nudging the man back against the big fender. "Show your weapons. And do it very carefully, one hiding place at a time."

"I told you, I got lost," the man repeated, rolling his eyes in frustration. "If I'm trespassing, I apologize." He looked over Shane's shoulder. "It's mighty lonesome out here."

"Stop the small talk." Shane put the gun to the man's heart. "I can always shoot you then frisk you, of course."

"All right. Okay." The man reluctantly did as Shane asked, revealing a pistol and a pocket knife. "I always carry a weapon. For personal protection."

"Throw your *personal protection* in the grass," Shane demanded.

The stranger did that, too, then glanced into the trees. "I thought I saw a woman in there, waving at me. Y'all need some help here?"

"As a matter of fact, we do," Shane replied, the gun still centered on the man's big chest. "We need you to take a message back to whoever sent you here. We have Timmy in custody and we will not let him go until *we* get some answers. If we don't get those answers, we'll turn him over to the local sheriff and let the great state of Texas do its own digging. But I'm guessing your boss wouldn't like that, now would he? *Or she?*"

The man's bushy bronzed-colored eyebrows lifted. "I don't know what you're talking about, Mister. I told you I got off the main road and couldn't find my way back. What's going on here? Who are you looking for?"

"Let me see your identification," Shane said, motioning to the man's coat pocket. "And be very careful about reaching for it."

The stranger let out a string of curses, then slowly pulled out a wallet and handed it to Shane.

"Walter Rogers, private detective. From Austin, Texas. Imagine that. You're a disgrace to your industry, Mr. Rogers. And you won't have a P.I. license after this."

Kit couldn't wait any longer. She hurried through the broken fence and rushed up behind Shane, her revolver pointed toward the surprised captive. "Where is Trudy Pearson?"

Shane moved an inch, shielding her from the man. "Go back and stay there," he said over his shoulder, his tone brooking no argument. "And be a dove and put the gun down."

But Katherine wasn't listening. She nosed closer. "No. I won't hide like a coward. This man knows something and he's going to tell us, right?"

Shane lowered his head in frustration. "I was working on that part, darling."

The man seemed a bit amused, which only made Kit even madder. Waving the gun, she asked, "Where is she?"

"She'll soon be out of the picture," the man said, grinning. "And you will be too, if you don't cooperate and come back to Austin with me."

Kit went for him, but Shane blocked her with a strong arm around her waist. "Patience, luv." He pushed the gun into the man's gut. "You've not only given us some very concrete information but you've upset her so I suggest you answer her. She knows how to use that revolver."

Then he whispered to Katherine, "We have our guns on him, now don't we? So no need to do anything rash."

She didn't care about that right now. She just wanted to tear this man's eyes out. "You won't get away."

"You do have me cornered," the man replied, laughing over at Shane. "Big gun aimed at my heart and big-shot woman to protect." Then he lifted one hand. "But *we* have even more big guns."

And then two more men stepped out of the trees on the other side of the road.

Kit gasped, but kept her weapon aimed steadily toward the man by the truck. She wouldn't go down without a good fight.

Shane leaned close to her, his eyes on the other men.

"Careful. They do have big guns. And since you insisted on coming to the party, you'd better do exactly as I say."

Kit really should have done what Shane had told her to do. *Stayed hidden.* But she thought with mutinous relief, if she'd stayed behind, she'd have been forced to ride back to the ranch alone. While these thugs loaded Shane onto the truck.

After a few minutes of a tense standoff where the two thugs advanced toward Shane and her, Rogers had finally told Shane that if they didn't throw down their weapons, he'd signal the sharpshooters waiting on a nearby hill. To kill the woman first.

So reluctantly, Shane had dropped his gun and motioned for her to do the same. And now they were on the back of the truck, getting wet while the two new-comers held them captive.

At least this way, she was here with him. And that meant these creeps couldn't use yet another person she cared about as a bargaining chip to get to her.

Then, in spite of the rain coming down on them, in spite of the two big men holding guns on them, in spite of it all, she realized she did care about Shane. A lot. And he'd kissed her back there underneath that tree in a way that told her he might just feel the same.

"Shane?" she whispered now, her mouth hardly moving.

Shane shot a covert smile toward the two solemn henchmen sitting on the truck with them. "Yes, my dear."

"I'm not sorry. I wouldn't have let them take you anyway. Not without me. I'd have come after you."

"That brings me a great deal of comfort, Kit," he replied, his own lips tightly drawn. "But the thing is, now I have to worry about keeping you alive."

"We can worry about each other," she said back.

She wanted to add more, much more to her declaration but one of the men grunted and pointed his nasty looking semiautomatic rifle toward them. "No talking."

Shane gave the man a serene smile. "So sorry. Did we bother you with our chatter?"

"Hey, I said no talking and I mean it. I'll put a gag on *her* if you say another word. And I'll take pleasure in doing it."

The look he sent Katherine made her shiver even while she stared him down. The look Shane shot her gave her courage, however.

Shane nodded to the man, his expression bordering on brutal even while he smiled.

"Sir, can I ask you something?" Katherine said in her best feminine voice, her eyes wide with an exaggerated concern.

The big man pushed at his wet, balding head, his fat fingers dragging through a few strands of oily hair. "What?"

"Where are we going?"

"Nice try, lady."

"It's a fair question, don't you think?"

At her sweet question, Shane poked her then gave her a warning glare.

"Your friend thinks you need to pipe down, honey," the other man said. "You'll find out where we're going soon enough."

And she did. They were taking the road back to the

ranch house. She glanced over at Shane, her brow lifting in a question mark.

He sent her yet another warning look then glanced at their guards. He quickly mouthed "Wait."

She heard the message, looked up to make sure the Brothers Grimm hadn't seen it then told herself to relax and let Shane handle this. Only she couldn't relax. So she started looking for ways to end this without getting herself or Shane shot, hoping Shane was doing the same on his side of the big, roaring truck.

He was.

The way Shane figured it, they would take them back to the house, kill him and probably everyone else, including their own mule Timmy, then take Katherine to the person who was waiting for all of this to happen.

And right now, Shane couldn't be sure if that person was a man or a woman.

His fired-up gut told him their nemesis could very well be a woman. Maybe even Kit's own best friend, Trudy Pearson.

What a dilemma. How could he convince Katherine that she might be in danger from a woman she'd trusted for so long? He'd have to worry about that little problem later. Right now, Shane had to figure out how to knock both these men off the truck and overtake the driver without getting Katherine killed in the process.

He had several things in his favor. One, the truck was wet and slick from the continuing rain. Traction would be at a minimum. Two, these two didn't look as sharp as they pretended to be. They looked downright confused and dazed, as if they hadn't signed up to hurt a woman. Three, they had left the horses grazing freely but Hercules would sense something was wrong and hopefully hightail it for home with the loyal Peaches following him. That would alert Nina and Paco that something was up. And four, if he could make Katherine understand his intentions, she just might save herself by helping him out a bit.

So he sat silent, calculating the distance to the house, calculating the distance and energy it would take for him to butt the bigger of the two off the side of the truck and grab the other one's gun at the same time and turn it on both the fallen men and the driver. He'd have to work fast and make sure he didn't get shot. If that happened, they'd finish him off and take Katherine away immediately.

Then he remembered the deep rut in the road about two miles from the main gate. Watching the bored men sitting on each side of the wide truck bed, Shane touched a finger to Katherine's arm but stared straight ahead. She took the hint and did the same, motioning back to him. He held her hand in his, tapped three times and prayed she'd get the message that on the count of three he aimed to get this fight started. When she glanced up he shifted his head toward the man on his side then looked over toward the muddy ditch.

She seemed to understand. She circled a finger in his palm, spelling out a number and letters that seemed to say "On 3? Got it."

The touch of her fingers tickling his skin, Shane wrote back "Y-e-s."

Then he waited, watching for the familiar turns on the muddy dirt road. Once he was sure they were approaching the dip that would be a full-blown mudhole by now with all the rain, he sent Katherine a quick glance, followed by a curt nod.

He stared straight ahead, waiting for the moment he could make his move. When he saw the road changing and recognized the curve, he winked at Katherine and tapped her palm again.

She took a long breath and gave him a covert lifting of her eyebrows, her hand squeezing his.

Shane looked up at the man nearest him, leaned up to stare past the man and shouted, "Did you see that?"

The man turned at about the same time the truck dipped to go through the mudhole and that's when Shane head-butted him in his midsection, making sure to grab the man's rifle before the poor soul tumbled over the truck's side. Before he could turn toward the now-surprised other guard, however, Katherine managed to use the shift in the truck to rise up enough to give the man a big shove, her deep grunt indicating how much energy she used to do so.

He went over the side, losing his gun as he joined his shocked buddy in the mud. Katherine held onto the side of the truck, her breath heaving as they watched the confused man give a valiant try to reaching for his soaked weapon. Shane shot him and ended that quest. Then even as the driver brought the truck to a halt in the middle of the big mudhole, Shane pumped a bullet into the first man who'd fallen into the mud.

"Stay down," he shouted at Katherine as he whirled toward the driver who was trying to emerge from the truck.

But Shane didn't get a chance to take down the driver. Another shot rang out from the nearby woods and the driver fell out the door face first into the mud.

It was over. The silence of the countryside screamed relief even as the echoes of the last gunshot vibrated through the trees. But where were the other sharpshooters the men had mentioned? And how many of them were there?

"Katherine?"

"I'm all right," she said, her hand reaching for his.

"Stay there," he said, lifting her hand to kiss her fingers then pushing her back down.

Shane realized the rain had ended. And he realized they were alive, but they were not alone. He heard a motor revving up.

"More?" Katherine asked from her spot in the bottom of the wet truck. "They said they had others posted on the hills, right?"

"I hope not," Shane said, squinting toward the overbearing noise. "I don't have enough ammunition to hold them off." Lifting her up, he said, "Let's get in the truck. We'll try to outrun them somehow."

He quickly lifted Kit over the side of the truck then pushed her toward the open door of the cab.

"Shane?" She pointed up the lane.

A man on a massive, shiny black motorcycle flew down the road toward them, coming from the direction of the ranch. A man on Shane's very own massive, shiny black motorcycle.

And he had a big gun, too.

THIRTEEN

Shane kept Kit there behind the truck door. "Hold on."

"But he's coming right at us," she shouted over the roar of the growling motorcycle.

"Yes, and just in time, too," Shane said, a grin splitting his face.

Thinking he'd somehow lost touch with reality, Katherine stared at Shane then looked at the approaching monster bike. "Shane, what's going on?"

Shane didn't answer. Instead, he dragged her around the truck and waited for the man to pull the sleek machine up next to them, the big tires spewing out a whirl of mud and wet rocks.

Shocked, Katherine instinctively moved closer to Shane while the man on the motorcycle lifted off, his weapon still intact, looked around at the carnage, then nodded to Shane. "Guess you didn't need my help out here after all, Knight."

Shane actually chuckled out loud. "We managed to take care of this mess," he said. "But why aren't you at the house interrogating our friend?"

"Been there, took care of that," the man said, his black

eyes moving over Katherine with a keen appraisal. "Oh, by the way, I borrowed your bike. Is this the client?"

Shane pulled Katherine to his side. "Yes. Katherine Barton Atkins, I'd like you to meet Luke 'Paco' Martinez, better known as the Warrior."

Katherine looked from Shane to the big man standing in front of her. Everything about the Warrior shouted darkness. His hair was the color of midnight dark chocolate. His eyes weren't very far behind, almost onyx. Even his skin was bronzed to a rich deep tan that looked as chiseled as a rock face and just about as hard and impenetrable. He held the heavy, nasty-looking rifle with an arm that rippled with firm muscles, his stance as fierce and determined as any ancient warrior she'd ever seen in books and on the big screen.

"Hello, Mr. Martinez," she said, her voice just above a squeak, or so it seemed to her ringing ears. "Thanks for coming."

"My job," the man replied, walking around the truck to check on the two unconscious men in the mud. "One's dead and one's still breathing," he reported back in a growling voice. Then he went to the ditch and checked the unconscious driver. "He's a goner, too."

"Had to be done," Shane replied. He turned to Katherine. "Paco is a trained sniper."

Paco watched her face as if to say "Does that scare you, lady?"

A chill went down Katherine's back. She could very well see that with her own eyes. "Again, thank you," she said, thinking how strange to be thanking someone for killing another human being. Her answer apparently worked. The man stopped glaring at her.

Paco looked from her back to Shane. "Hey, I took

care of two other shooters, in case you were wondering," he said, his tone all business. "Found them on my way in, hovering up on that north ridge." He pointed off toward the curve leading to the main gate. "Probably planned to take you out then once they had the woman, move on into the house and finish off everyone there. But they're all trussed up and waiting for the authorities. Had to talk myself out of shooting 'em."

Katherine gulped a breath, hearing him describe in such a monotone, matter-of-fact way how things might have ended up here. She said a quick prayer of thanks, her stomach roiling in sick waves, the heaviness of death all around her.

"I owe you yet again, my friend," Shane said, shaking Paco's big hand. "And our young Timmy?"

"Timmy can get pretty chatty when he sets his mind to it," Paco replied, his face as blank as a slab of marble. "I got some stuff we might be able to use. He's still kinda tied up, waiting for you."

"Let's get this cleaned up," Shane said, turning grim and serious. "We'll discuss this at the house."

Paco nodded, the movement curt and without an inch of waste. "Take her on back. I'll deal with this."

Shane looked at Katherine. "Good idea. She's too exposed out here in the open."

Paco didn't respond. He simply went over to the still-alive man and frisked him with the agility of a magician. Then he did the same with the two dead men. "Go," he finally said to Shane, a sleek phone in one hand.

Shane urged Katherine ahead of him. "We'll have to walk. The truck is evidence." He turned to face his friend again. "How'd you know to come, Paco?"

Paco stood up, grunted. "Hercules. He came galloping

up to the house and whinnied. Had a cute little mare with him. It was annoying. Figured that stallion wouldn't shut up until I did something." He pointed toward the big bike. "Found this out in the stables and tracked y'all to the fence line. Saw a lot of muddy tracks all along the road, did some snooping around. That's when I spotted the snipers up on the ridge."

Shane nodded. "So you arrived undetected, interrogated Timmy, then tracked the sharpshooters first and came here and found us."

"Something like that." Paco sent Katherine a hard look then turned away. "I came in through the river."

"He doesn't discuss his methods," Shane whispered as he helped Katherine along the road.

"I don't want to know anyway," she said, all sorts of horrible images running through her head. But she couldn't help but turn and watch as Paco Martinez made fast work of securing the bodies. "What…what will become of the ones who survived?"

Shane glanced around. "Paco will call the authorities, explain the situation, and get the injured man medical attention right away. The other two will have some explaining to do."

"And the dead?"

"Will be identified, sent home and hopefully given a proper burial."

"Just like that. Two men dead and it's all so cut-and-dried?"

He watched her face, probably waiting for some sort of feminine hysteria to kick in. But she didn't give him any theatrics. She was too numb and tired to care if all of the CHAIM agents were trained to read body language.

"It's never cut-and-dried, Kit. Those men came here to kill my entire staff and me, and probably young Timmy, too. They wanted to take you. And they nearly succeeded. I should never have taken you out there with me."

"But if you hadn't, you might be dead right now and they would have found everyone inside the house anyway."

He didn't respond to that. He kept on walking, his gaze darting here and there. While Katherine tried to imagine what she would have done if they had killed him.

"They'll go over this truck for prints, anything that might help us."

"Thank you," she finally said, aware that he was trying to maintain his professionalism to block the real issues here. "You've saved me yet again." She gave him a questioning stare. "You'll be taking me back to Austin now, right? So we can find Trudy?"

Shane slowly guided her through the ruts and mud. "I can't take you back there yet. It's too dangerous. And it might be too late."

The implication of his words hit her full force. "You mean, too late for Trudy. They did say if I didn't come out of hiding, they'd kill her."

"Yes, they did say that. But we can't base anything on such threats. And you are my first concern. They're waiting to hear from their man and…he won't ever talk again."

"So you're just going to keep me here and let them kill Trudy?"

He looked straight ahead. "As I said, you are my first priority."

Kit was so mad she seriously thought about making a run for the highway. But then she wouldn't be able to strangle Shane Warwick. Yes, he'd saved her life, but he'd also manipulated her into believing he would help Trudy.

"Shane?"

"Remember, I have people looking for your friend already. No need for you to get involved in that right now."

She did remember that, and she remembered hugging him tight and telling him she'd have to learn to trust him. But still, she couldn't help but be furious that he refused to take her home.

"You tricked me. You said you needed to talk to that driver to find out more information. And now he's dead."

"No, I did not trick you. I did what I had to do to keep you safe."

"But we didn't find out anything more than we already knew. I want to go to Austin."

He sent her an indulgent look, which only infuriated her further. "They don't have her in Austin."

"Oh, so you know where they're holding her even though you never got that information out of any of those men back there?"

"No, but I can lay odds it's not in Austin. Too obvious."

Well, she hadn't considered that but because she was still angry with him and everyone else involved in this, she wanted to fight a bit more. "Shouldn't we start there and see?"

"First things first," he said, his tone so patently patient, she wanted to scream. "We get all of this cleared up with the local authorities, we get you to a new location, then we try to find out about that little black phone. Meantime, Paco has worked on our little Timmy and he'll give me a full report. And we still have the authorities in Austin holding the shooter in custody. He won't be going anywhere for a while since he tried to shoot up a room full of people and we have hundreds of witnesses. The people who sent him have to stay well hidden for now. That's why they sent Timmy here.

"Timmy, bless him, is too stupid to do more than whine out a few hints however. They probably made sure he was completely confused and unreliable in the memory department and they put a huge fear in his heart, so he might not have given Paco much to work with. We'll have to turn him over to the local authorities and explain he was trespassing and that he threatened us with a weapon. That should hold him in a secure spot for a long time. So that leaves your friend Trudy."

"How will we find her?"

"I'm working on that." He hurried along, constantly checking the trees and pastures. "Kit, please understand me. I had no choice but to kill those men. If they'd accomplished what they came to do, you'd be headed to a fate I can't even begin to describe. It was the only way. They obviously put some sort of GPS tracker on that phone they had Timmy hand deliver so we don't have much time. We have to find out how they found us in the first place then we have to move you. Do you trust me to do that?"

"I'm trying," she said, some of her anger dissipating in view of his fierce protectiveness and that sure fate he'd saved her from. "I'm worried about Trudy. She shouldn't have to pay for my problems."

"We'll find her," he said, his hand touching hers for a brief second.

Kit watched his face, wondering how the man never managed to break a sweat. His dark hair was sleek and crisp, as fresh as dark coffee in spite of being damp. His eyes, so crystalline and challenging, held no hint of all the turmoil surrounding them. And even in a dirty button-down casual shirt, jeans and expensive cowboy boots now caked in mud, he still exuded the markings of a man born to wear a tuxedo.

While she on the other hand felt aged and frazzled, tired and ragged, in her own filthy short-sleeved sweater and damp old blue jeans, her hair falling out of the loose clip she'd tried to secure it with earlier. Kit supposed it didn't matter very much what one wore on the run, but... she couldn't help remembering the feeling of being all dressed up and in Shane's arms, before all the terror began.

If she survived this, would she ever get that chance again? Did she want that? To be in his arms, dancing?

And what did it matter now? She was supposed to be mad at the man, not daydreaming about dancing with him. But she realized she was misdirecting this anger toward the one person who was on her side—Shane Warwick. She'd just witnessed the kind of violence that made her sick to her stomach. She should be praying for Trudy's safe return and praying for those poor men back there, dead or alive. So she did say her prayers and she included *this* infuriating man in those prayers. How could she be mad at him for doing the best he could to protect her?

Dear Lord, help me to remember all the good in this man. Such as his kiss and his honor.

"What are you thinking over there?" he asked, as if he knew her thoughts.

She didn't dare tell him the whole truth. "Nothing. Prayers for everyone involved in this and just remembering my life before. It seems like a dream now."

"Why don't you tell me about it?" he asked, smiling over at her as they approached the open gate to the main house. Seeing her distress, he said, "Paco left the gate open for us. Now, back to your life before?"

"I've told you a lot about my past already. Are you hoping maybe I'll give you some more hints?"

"Well, there is that to consider, luv. But I'd really like to hear about your life, because, work aside, I'd like to know more about you."

She stretched, gazing out at the dark morning sky. "I might bore you, although my life has been anything but normal lately."

"You, my love, could never bore me."

The way he said that made her body turn all soft, made her heart flutter like a trapped bird. She knew the endearment was second nature to such a charmer, that he probably hadn't even realized he'd said it. And yet, his words lingered over her like a soft shield, making her feel safe and secure. Why had she been so angry earlier? She had no reason to blame all of this on Shane. Maybe her anger was misplaced to protect her battered heart.

She glanced over at him, her whole being softening to him yet again. He made her feel as if they could get through anything together. He gave her hope and showed her how to trust again. And she knew in her heart she was finally ready to talk to him about her life up until now. Even the parts she'd never talked about to anyone.

He held her back when they reached the house. After searching the yard and looking around, he said, "I want to hear everything about you, Kit, and not because I'm fishing for information. I want to know about your life because I like hearing about *you*. You're an amazing woman."

She glanced around, her gaze taking in the beautiful old house and the surrounding land. The rain dripped in a slow cadence off the tiled roof, making her wish they could curl up together on the couch and really talk. "But you have things to take care of right now."

"Yes, I do," he said, his hand reaching up to touch her disheveled hair. "Let me get to the task at hand while you freshen up and get some rest." Then he leaned close, a soft smile covering his face. "I'll make a deal with you. I'll tell you everything I can find out about Trudy and these people who are after you and you can tell me everything about you and your life."

Kit basked in the radiance of his beautiful eyes, letting the warmth of his nearness hold her for one brief blissful moment. She wanted to kiss him again. "Shane—"

"Not now, luv." He touched a finger to her nose. "Not now. Too much between us." His finger moved with a featherlike caress across her cheekbone. "Later, my dear Kit. Later, we will get to know each other on a proper date. I promise. Just a brief interlude before we go back into the fray. Or if not, then definitely after."

Kit would hold him to that promise. If they could even hope to have a proper date now or after this was over. "I'll be there," she said in a whisper.

He smiled, kissed her cheek and said, "And maybe you can wear that lovely dress you had on the other night."

"No," she said. "I don't want to wear that dress ever again. But I will dress up."

"I don't care what you wear, just so I can know you're safe once and for all."

And with that, he gave her a peck on the cheek. "Now inside with you. I'll go in with you and check to make sure everyone is safe and accounted for then I'll have to do a walkabout around the property."

His cell rang. Still watching her, he touched the screen to answer. "Warwick." Listening, he kept his eyes on her.

Kit turned toward the house, her mind humming with all sorts of contradictory thoughts about the man who both frightened and endeared her. But she had to wonder where this relationship would go once the threat of evil was behind them.

Before she could form another thought, Shane grabbed her and put a finger to his lips, pulling her back toward the garage, his whisper near her ear. "We've got more trouble. The Warrior didn't make the kill shot on the driver. Someone else did. He found casings that don't match any of our weapons. And he thinks whoever did it might be in the house waiting for us."

FOURTEEN

Kit inhaled a haggard breath. "No. No, Shane. What about Nina and—"

He silenced her with a shake of his head. "We have to get in there and find out."

Kit tried to block the horrible images running through her head. If something had happened to Shane's family here--the people he loved—she'd never forgive herself. "Let's go."

"Don't make a sound, no matter what you see or hear," he told her, his hand holding tightly to her while he shielded her body with his. He had his gun back, but she'd left hers behind after those men had taken them.

Slowly, with hardly a sound, Shane clicked open the back door leading into the kitchen. Pushing Kit behind him, he whirled with his gun drawn, his gaze moving with computer-like efficiency across the room. "Clear," he said, motioning for her to stay behind him.

Kit looked around, shock expelling in every rapid breath. "They've ransacked your house."

"Yes, I can see that," Shane whispered as they skirted around broken dishes and open cabinet doors.

Kit followed him through the first level of the house as they entered room after room. And in each room, drawers had been opened, contents spilled out, books had been thrown off shelves and pictures ripped from the walls. They finally made it to the back of the house where Shane's office door stood open. "Stay back," he said, pushing her to the side as he pivoted into the room.

Kit didn't know whether to look or not. A heavy dread held her down, clutching her in a grip of sheer terror. And when Shane emerged from the room, his expression grim and dark, she knew that dread was right on target. "What?" she asked, her hand grabbing his arm.

"Timmy is dead," he whispered, shaking his head. "One shot through the forehead. And the office is a mess."

Kit gasped and put a hand to her mouth. "Oh, no. Oh, no." Then she touched his shirt. "Where is everyone else?"

"I don't know," Shane whispered, a hand on her arm. "But they know the rules. They should have managed to hide."

"How can we find them?"

He didn't answer. Pulling his phone out, he touched the screen and put the phone to his ear, waiting. Then he breathed a sigh of relief. "Nina, where are you?"

Kit's heart pulsed into overdrive. Nina was safe and hopefully that meant that Ricardo and Silvia were, too.

"Stay put," Shane replied. "I'm going to make sure the house is secure."

At her questioning look, he said, "Ricardo was guarding Timmy when he heard the intruder. He decided to protect his family—smart move. They managed to get out of the house and hide out in the barn. We have a safe room out there under the floor for tornadoes and other dangers. We've rarely had to use it, but thank goodness Nina thought about it today."

A safe room. Kit shuddered again, chills warring with heat throughout her body. She imagined that's where she'd be stuffed if Shane thought it would protect her. She followed him up the stairs, her thoughts on the dead man downstairs. It was all too much, just too much. She didn't think she could make it up the stairs. Every ounce of energy she had left seemed to drain right out of her system.

Shane turned, sensing her hesitation. "Kit?"

"I'm dizzy," she said, grabbing the railing. "Just go. I'll wait here."

"No." He pulled her close, his gaze locking with hers, his eyes soft and gentle. "Don't give up on me now. You're safe. You're alive."

She held her head down, her hands gripping the railing. "But for how long? And how many more have to die in order for you to save me?"

"Kit, look at me."

She lifted her head and saw the concern in his eyes. This was different from the first night she'd met him. Today, his concern was soaked in some other emotion that matched what she was feeling in her heart. "I'll be okay. It's just so horrible. And senseless. It makes me so mad I can't function!"

He held a hand to her chin. "I'm going to get you out of this, I promise."

"But so many people are dead." Her eyes burned with the hysteria she'd held at bay for days now. "Dead, Shane, because of me, because of something they think I have, or some kind of information they want me to give them. And I don't know what they want. I don't know anything and I don't have anything."

"C'mon," he said, tugging her close. "Just hang on until I can make sure we're alone."

She managed a deep, calming breath, his strength, his warmth, helping her to get her bearings again. Clutching her pearls like a lifeline, she said, "I'm all right." But she wondered if she'd ever be all right again. What did these people want from her?

Dear God, please help us. Please help Shane find out the truth.

They checked every room in the house and found no one. The culprit had accomplished his main objective and now he was long gone. The intruder hadn't found anything but he'd done his best to destroy the whole house.

Shane called Paco to give him an update. "I think one of them got away."

Kit had to wonder when the next one would show up.

"You were right," she said after Shane called Nina to tell her it was safe. "They killed Timmy just as you said they would."

Shane nodded, his expression grim. "Yes, not only did they kill him but they took out their own man there on the road. He'd compromised them with that little run-in with us."

"But they had us. They could have taken me."

"Instead, they tried to bring us back to the house," Shane replied, his confusion measured against the calm in his eyes. "Someone instructed that sniper to finish off the last man standing, which means Paco missed a man when he subdued the two on the ridge. Why didn't the last man try to take out Paco or us when he killed his own man?"

"Do you think he panicked?"

"Possibly," he replied as they made it back to the kitchen. "Or maybe his superiors thought we had evidence here at the house. That would mean one of them came here after Paco left, killed Timmy and searched the office." He ran a hand through his hair. "The plan was for Timmy to meet the driver at the designated location and when he didn't show, they knew things had gone bad. So they took out Timmy and the driver after we'd already shot the other two. That eliminates any witnesses."

"Except us."

"Someone set out to kill you but now they want you very much alive, luv."

Kit shuddered again, her eyes going wide. "But they let you live, too, Shane."

"Yes, they did." He gave her a level look. "Which means they need both of us alive now. Just until they have what they want. Based on what they did to this place, they must think you've told me something very incriminating." Then he tugged her close, his expression hard. "But you haven't now, have you?"

Kit sat by the window in the big den, her mind reeling with Shane's earlier question. Did he actually think she was keeping information from him?

After helping Nina and Ricardo straighten what they could of the messy house, she'd been waiting here with Silvia for two hours and now it was growing dark outside. In spite of Silvia's stoic comments here and there and the bright security lights surrounding the house, each shifting shadow made her shiver. She'd been jittery all day long. No, she'd been jittery since that night at the gala. And she had to wonder what Shane and Paco were discussing behind the closed door of his office.

Closing her eyes to the memory of the coroner coming to remove Timmy's body, she wondered what Shane had told the big, burly Texas Ranger who'd shown up to get a statement from all of them. While she understood CHAIM had operatives in all sorts of law enforcement quarters, she also knew those operatives were trained to stay inside the law and to always call in the proper authorities for assistance on any mission. Still, it was never wise to mess with a Ranger. But whatever they'd discussed in Shane's office, the man had tipped his hat and left without getting a statement from her. Did elite private security spies trump everything as a means to an end? Or had her name and status allowed her a reprieve from any further interrogations?

And when would Shane ever come out of that office and talk to her?

Earlier, after they'd made sure Nina and the others were safe, Shane escorted her to her door. After checking the room and clearing up some of the spilled contents of the dressers and closet, he'd told her to rest.

"But—"

"We'll discuss everything later."

His brusque manner of dismissing her had left Kit confused and angry. Had he suspected her all along of harboring some sort of information that could solve this?

As if I wouldn't tell him that right away, if I had anything to tell.

She got up and paced around the room, eyeing the many books she'd helped return to the long shelf across one wall. When her gaze hit on an old Bible, Kit pulled it off the shelf and sank into a leather chair. Leafing through the pages, she hoped to gain some comfort from the Scriptures.

"Read it out loud, *querida*," Silvia said.

"But select capable men from all the people—men who fear God, trustworthy men who hate dishonest gain—and appoint them as officials over thousands, hundreds, fifties and tens." The verse from Exodus seemed to leap off the page at Kit.

Silvia nodded her approval. "Shane is such a man."

Shane was such a man. He was trustworthy and he hated dishonest gain, but he was also a trained operative who went after criminals with a vigilante force. Did that make all the death surrounding her tonight right? Was all of this justified in order to save her from some sort of evil?

And Jacob. He'd been trustworthy once. But something had happened to her husband. Had Jacob done something for dishonest gain? Had he used her trips to Mexico to hide something else? Had she blocked something out along with the pain of his death? And the pain of his rejection?

Tears pricking her eyes, Kit went back to reading the Bible, hoping God's word would trigger some sort of distant memory that could unlock the puzzle she'd somehow become involved in. She stopped in Proverbs this time, chapter 16, verse 11—"The Lord demands accurate scales and balances; he sets the standards for fairness."

Balances. Fairness.

Silvia stopped her knitting. "Good over evil, always."

Kit's heart pounded a heavy beat. Memories of Jacob behind the closed door of his office, just as Shane was now, came into her mind with kaleidoscope clarity. His voice had risen in anger as he told the person on the other end of the line that the balance wasn't adding up.

Balance of what?

Jacob had never discussed his work with her, other than in general terms. She learned more at dinner parties about his commitment to Texas and his many holdings than she did during dinner when it was just the two of them.

Dropping the Bible on the table by her chair, Kit put a hand to her pearls. Maybe she *had* been hiding the truth from Shane…and from herself. She and Jacob had drifted apart over the years but she'd refused to face that. She'd wanted children while he kept coming up with excuses to wait. She'd wanted a more simple life while he thrived on the spotlight. Jacob demanded power, status and wealth while Kit tried so very hard not to make any demands on her husband. She'd buried herself in the foundation, hoping to help other children since she didn't have any of her own.

And she'd wanted her husband to come home on time and be with her when she knew in her heart he'd been spending time with another woman. Yet she'd never been able to prove her suspicions. Jacob had been good at hiding his indiscretions.

That was why he'd given her these pearls and taken her out to dinner. He'd tried to pacify her, to assure her she was the only woman in his life and that maybe it was time to start that family they talked about. And she'd believed him because she thought that was the only way she could keep him. Talk about standing by her man. She'd tried so hard.

Had he been lying to her even then?

"Kit?"

She turned, startled by her thoughts and by the man standing in the doorway staring at her with fathomless blue eyes. "Yes?"

Abuela Silvia gathered her things and silently left the room. Her sitter had been dismissed, Kit thought.

Shane came into the room and sat down across from her. "Are you all right?"

"Not really," she said, her confusion and pain making her words sharp. "I've been waiting here all evening." Sickening, how familiar that statement sounded. She'd certainly said that enough to her husband.

Shane, however, was not her husband. Not even close. "I'm sorry. I thought you'd still be resting."

"I did rest. And then I helped put this house back to order and I had dinner with Nina and Silvia. We need to talk, Shane."

"I know that," he said, rubbing his hand down his neck. "Paco thinks someone close to you managed to find out where you were located—some sort of tracking device maybe. We can't figure how or where they planted it. I checked your mother's car and it's clean. This place isn't even on the map and I was careful that we weren't being followed the other night."

"What else did he find out from Timmy?"

A dark wariness colored his gaze. "Mexico, again, luv. Timmy remembered hearing the man speaking on the phone about some sort of demands from someone in Mexico."

"I don't know what that could mean," she replied, hoping he'd believe her. "I only went down there on humanitarian trips, Shane. That's the truth."

"But your husband went with you on occasion."

"Yes, yes, he did. I can't speak for him."

"We'll start at the beginning again. Maybe we can find a clue if we both think back."

Kit saw the fatigue pulling at his face. "Where's Mr. Martinez now?"

"Checking the premises. The man never sleeps. And when he does, it's usually out under the stars."

Glad to have another subject to discuss for a brief minute, she said, "He's…interesting."

"That's a good word for it, yes." Shane put his hands down on his knees, his eyes holding hers. "Paco has Native American blood running through his veins. His great-grandfather was Apache. He comes from a family of soldiers and he can track anything that moves. He fights down and dirty, but he's terrified of any sort of intimate relationship with a woman. That's why he's so good at his job. He stays focused."

Kit felt the sting of that implication. "And you're not able to focus? Because you seem to thrive on relationships with women?"

He gave her a hard stare that moved through a shadow of emotions—empathy, need, longing, understanding and finally, regret. "I've had a lot of bad relationships with women, and yes, it does tend to become a distraction." He lowered his gaze. "Sometimes that kind of distraction can turn out tragically."

"Who was she?" Katherine asked, determined to learn more about him, too.

He pushed into the chair. "It was early on in my career. A spoiled college student. Her father was a diplomat. Two of us were assigned to escort her on a foreign tour. But I got distracted by her charms and she betrayed my trust. A tragic lesson well learned."

"I'm sorry," Katherine said. It was obvious that incident had colored his whole life. "But you stayed with CHAIM."

"Yes, after some intense training in Ireland—and to prove myself. Sometimes I think they assign me to beautiful women as a test." He leaned up. "And I don't intend to fail that test, Kit. Not with you."

"Am I now a distraction? Because you're attracted to me and yet you think I'm hiding something from you?"

His body jolted, his eyes going dark. "I lost someone I cared about because I let my heart get ahead of my focus. I wasn't as experienced then. I am experienced now—in both combat and in matters of the heart. I'm here to protect you. End of discussion."

Shocked, she saw it all there at last. He wasn't such a player after all. He was terrified of giving himself over to his feelings. "Are you afraid you'll fail again, Shane?"

He ignored that last question. "Are you hiding something?"

How like him to answer all of her questions with one of his own. "Is this an interrogation?"

He sank back in the chair. "No. I don't want to interrogate you. But Paco and I have gone over every bit of information we could find on you and your husband—thankfully I destroyed most of it and the rest is locked up in a secure cabinet—and downloaded to my phone—so our intruders didn't get to it. Everything looks clean. But looks can be deceiving, even on paper. I'm beginning to think you actually *don't* know the whole truth."

She swallowed back the choking dread in her throat. "Maybe I didn't want to see the whole truth."

He watched as she fidgeted with her pearls then moved her hand over her gold bracelet watch. "Would you like to talk about it? We did agree to do that, remember?"

"I remember. And if I'm honest with you, will you be honest with me?"

His dark eyebrows shot up. "About what?"

She leaned forward, her fingers touching together. "I want to know everything good or bad you've found regarding my husband. I need to know the truth, so I can move on with my life. That is if I live to see another day. But I also need you to trust me, show me that you believe in me. So be honest with me. Don't hold anything back. I can't take that again, ever."

He was up and out of the chair in an instant, pulling her close to stare down at her. "Oh, you'll live another day, darling. You'll live a lifetime. I intend to see to that. And whatever happened between you and your husband won't happen between us. Because I would never neglect nor betray a woman like you."

So he did know some of her secrets after all.

And she needed to know some of his. "Is there something happening between us?"

"In spite of my best intentions otherwise, I do believe so."

"This person you cared about—it was the young woman?"

His smile betrayed the truth. "No, it was another CHAIM agent—a fellow rookie. The woman I thought I loved turned out to be a ruthless killer—an extremist with misguided intentions. She took his life to punish me. And I made sure she paid dearly for it."

Kit held a hand to her mouth. "That's not what I expected." Then she lifted her gaze to his, honesty her only weapon. "I'm not that woman, Shane. I'm just the widow of a powerful man who stopped loving me long before he died."

The expression in his eyes changed, went dark. "And I'm just the man who's beginning to care about you too much."

"What are you going to do about it?"

"For starters, this."

He reached for her and kissed her long and hard, with a tenderness that left her breathless and confused. Then he lifted his head, his eyes bright with longing. "And in spite of my intentions otherwise, I want to keep kissing you until I figure it out."

Kit pulled away, her pulse doing a rapid dance. "You don't trust me and yet, you just kissed me. You said yourself you've been down this road before."

"No, never *this* road. Never feeling the way I do with you." His eyes traced a path over her face. "There's a big difference between a kiss and a deep, abiding trust, luv. Trust makes things that much sweeter."

She stepped back. "So your kiss means nothing even though you say you've never felt like this before? Is it a means to get me to relax and talk?"

He tugged her back again, one hand around her waist.

"Kissing you, dear Kit, means more than I can say. And that's what scares me the most."

"Then stop kissing me and let me tell you the story of my marriage."

He moved a hand down her hair, his fingers touching on her pearls. "The real story?"

"Yes," she said, closing her eyes to the gentleness of his touch dancing over her skin. "But not the story of secrets and shady dealings. The real story of how our marriage was falling apart, piece by piece, and how I let it happen. Maybe in doing so, we can find out the truth about who's trying to kill me, and then you'll see that I have nothing to hide. Except a broken heart."

FIFTEEN

Shane sat there in the quiet, dark room, listening to the beautiful woman sitting across from him as she poured her heart out. It wasn't easy, listening to someone's deep, dark secrets, watching the slash of pain expressed with each word, each memory. But sometimes, with this job, it came with the territory. Devon Malone would know how to counsel Kit right now. Devon was a minister in every sense of the word. The man had always been a minister first and a special operative second. It was in Devon's blood to help those who needed counseling and solace.

It was in Shane's blood to make the bad guys suffer. That was his mode of operation. Get in. Get the bad guys. Maybe fall for a pretty face. And move to the next assignment. He'd known going in that protecting a beautiful woman would be his downfall, but he usually handled the situation with a light touch. And Kit was so right; it wasn't as if he hadn't been here before.

Only this time, with this particular woman, was different. She was different. She was real. Real in her faith, real in her devotion to her charitable works and real in her sense of loyalty to those she loved.

This time he'd fallen hard. So hard that he intended

to get to the bottom of things with this bizarre case so he could be with the woman free and clear. And maybe forever.

"I loved him so much," she said now, her green eyes as deep and rich as the ferns growing underneath the cottonwood trees out on the stream. "I wanted to be the best wife possible." She shrugged, the movement causing her shimmering hair to shift over the soft blue scarf covering her shoulders. "It was a matter of pride and propriety, you see. I'm a Barton, after all. Everything had to be perfect—at least on the surface. And we had the perfect marriage—the success, the looks, the big house in the exclusive neighborhood, the same seats on a front pew each Sunday. We were the 'it' couple for many years."

She stopped, her hands wrung together in her lap. "He did go on several trips with me and he seemed genuinely interested in my work at the foundation."

"When you were down in Mexico, did he disappear sometimes? Go off by himself?"

"Yes." She lowered her head. "I had my suspicions, but it has nothing to do with business deals. I didn't question him. I was too glad to have him there with me."

"And then?"

"And then, the power and control overtook the love and the vows we made to each other. Jacob had high aspirations while I wanted to have a family. We argued a lot. He didn't come home on time. He hated going to church and only attended so he'd be seen as a fine, upstanding man. Sometimes, he'd stay in town in the apartment he rented near the capital." She looked up then and straight into Shane's eyes. "And I'm pretty sure he didn't always stay there alone."

"He was unfaithful?"

She nodded and lowered her head, her obvious disgust and shame breaking Shane's heart. "I could never be sure. But a woman always knows these things, doesn't she?"

Shane couldn't answer that question. But he had his own suspicions regarding Jacob Atkins's less than stellar reputation. When he remembered all the women he'd thought he loved and left, he felt that same intense shame, too. "What made you think your husband was having an affair?"

She laughed, a curt little shattering laugh. "Oh, there were a hundred clues. His late nights away from me. His excuses for staying in the city. The way he'd sit staring off into space at the breakfast table or take phone calls in another room. The way he'd lavish me with gifts and promise me one day we'd have that family I wanted."

She reached up, twisting her pearls around her finger, her wedding ring shining with diamonds. "He gave me these pearls the last time I saw him. I had accused him earlier that week of deliberately pulling away from me because he had someone else, so he came home early and we had a wonderful dinner. He swore to me he'd never do anything to hurt me and that he loved me. Then he made me promise I'd always wear these pearls, for him." Her smile was full of pain. "But he never actually told me the truth. Jacob had a way of spinning things, a way of making me think I was all wrong, that I'd imagined everything."

Letting go of the pearls, she shook her head. "I honestly think that's why I kept denying I was in danger after he died. I wanted to keep the image of our perfect marriage intact in spite of the ugly letters and strange phone calls I started receiving. Even dead, my husband messed with my head to the point that I couldn't make coherent decisions regarding my own safety. How pathetic is that?"

Shane refrained from taking her in his arms. He needed to take his own advice and focus on this case. Those letters and phone calls were the reason he'd been called in the first place. Every threat had to be taken seriously.

But right now, he needed to reassure her. "You are a good and decent woman, Katherine. You wanted to honor your marriage vows. And you wanted to do right in the world. There is nothing pathetic in that. I'd say it's very admirable."

"Admirable?" She hissed through a tight breath. "Admirable to let your husband lie to you over and over, to sit in church together with smiles on our faces knowing we were the worst kind of hypocrites? Admirable to ignore the whispers, the signs, the well-meaning suggestions of friends? But I refused to listen. I refused to accept the truth. And now, I think my denial has brought this on me. If I'd demanded answers, if I'd asked questions when he was still alive, I might have saved not only myself but my husband, too. Maybe he would have talked to me, asked for my help. But he didn't. He couldn't, because Jacob never included me in his business decisions or his life, for that matter." Her eyes caught Shane's in a tormented light. "Trudy tried to tell me, but I wouldn't even listen to my best friend."

Shane's pulse bumped through his system like a

warning beeper going into high alert mode. "Trudy knew about Jacob's affair?"

"She hinted at it, yes."

"When was this?"

Shocked, Kit frowned at him. "Right after her husband died. I went to see her, hoping to comfort her and when the conversation turned to Jacob, she told me I couldn't trust him. So we argued. I can't even remember half of what we said to each other except that she envied Jacob and me and told me I needed to quit taking him for granted. She said if I wanted to save my marriage, I'd better start paying more attention to my husband."

"But you obviously made up with her, reconciled things."

"Yes, we forgave each other when Jacob died. She came to the funeral and we sat and cried together. We're closer now than we've ever been." She held up her wrist, dangling her bracelet watch at him. "She took me out to dinner for my birthday and gave me this watch."

Shane's pulse went into a flatline. "When is your birthday, luv?"

"It was a little over a month ago," she replied, her frown increasing. "Why do you ask?"

Shane got up and grabbed her wrist. "I need to see that watch."

Without waiting for her to take it off, he managed to loosen the clasp and pull the delicate gold bracelet off her slender arm. Then he turned the watch over. "I'll need to take the back off it, if you don't mind."

"Of course I mind," she said, shooting up and out of her chair. "I'm trying to tell you what I've been through and you're worried about this watch?"

He nodded then took her hand in his. "Yes, I'm very

much worried about this watch. Because I think your friend Trudy put a GPS tracking chip in your birthday gift."

The look on Katherine's face moved from a confused frown to shocking, all-consuming anger. "You can't be serious!"

Shane held the watch in the air as if it were a snake. "Deadly serious. It explains everything. That's apparently how she kept tabs on you. And that's how she knew you were here with me. She probably panicked after the shooting since no one would tell her where you were. But she had this to locate you. And then she somehow managed to come up with a plan to find you. It's elaborate and hard to believe, but it was a plan to draw you out. She's pretending to be kidnapped, to bring you back."

Katherine stood behind her chair, holding on to it so hard her knuckles looked as if they'd crack. "They're *holding* her hostage, or did you forget that? Why do you insist on thinking the worst of her? You said you'd be honest with me but you haven't been at all. What do you think you know about Trudy Pearson, Shane?"

Before he could answer, Paco came bolting into the room. "Shane, the cell's ringing. And we can't get a trace. Kissie tried every way possible to break the encryption but we haven't managed yet."

He threw Shane the cheap black phone that had started this whole new chain of events. Shane had passed it to Paco earlier so Paco could coordinate things with Kissie to see if they might have a chance of tracing it. But he'd given Paco orders to bring the phone to him if they got any incoming calls.

Shane stared down at the phone then handed it to Kit.

"I think your best friend wants to talk to you, luv. Try to get as much information as possible from her. And please don't mention that we might be on to her."

Kit shot Shane a pointed look as she took the phone then tugged away when he tried to listen in. His frown shouted disapproval but his ridiculous conclusions made her want to knock him silly. She'd deal with that later. Right now, she wanted to hear Trudy's voice and know that her friend was safe. "Trudy? Where are you?"

A male voice rasped across the wire. "Oh, she's about six feet under right about now."

"What?" Kit's heart accelerated so rapidly, she reached for a chair to hold her up. "What are you saying? Where is Trudy? Put her on the phone right now!"

"Trudy can't come to the phone, ever again. You didn't follow our directions," the voice replied. "People are dead because of you. Including your feisty little red-headed friend."

"No. No." Kit looked around at Shane, anger merging with a deep dread throughout her system. Turning away from his questioning gaze, she screamed into the phone. "I want to talk to her!"

"Too late for Trudy. But if you listen to us and do not repeat our conversation, you might get to live after you give us the information we need. If you don't listen we will find someone else to take your place. For example, your parents are such a lovely couple. We see them in church every Sunday and we have it on good authority that they are no longer holed up at Eagle Rock. And you have several college students working for you this summer. We know where they all go to school and we know some of them stay at your lovely home in Austin while they intern. One of them could go missing." He paused then growled, "Or we could just take out Shane Warwick and end it all. Without his protection, you'd be easy to find. Are you ready to meet with us, Mrs. Atkins? Just answer yes or no, please."

Kit swallowed the bile rising to her throat. Could they be lying to her to draw her out? She couldn't take that chance. "Yes, I understand."

"I'll be in touch in a few hours. For the well-being of all involved, don't repeat this to your bodyguard."

The connection was lost, the phone line silent. "Hello?" Nothing. She frantically tried dialing the number back but no ring tones echoed through the line.

Finally, she turned to Shane, tears of rage forcing their way down her face, her whole body shuddering with grief and anger. "I hope you're satisfied."

"Katherine?"

Still gripping the phone, she lunged at Shane, her fist balled up like jagged barbed wire as she pounded his chest. "She's dead! Dead. They killed her! You wouldn't let me help her and now they've killed her." She glared up at him, her body shutting down with each beat of her pulse, her mind going numb with a death-like fusion of pain and despair as everything that had happened over the last few days finally and completely caught up with her.

Shane grabbed her wrist, holding her hands away as he watched her face, his eyes burning a raw, white-hot crystal. "What did they say? Was it a man or a woman?"

"A man," she replied, her control just beyond snapping. "He said Trudy was dead and if I didn't cooperate, I'd soon be too." She stopped, calculating how much to tell him. She wouldn't reveal anything to Shane because Shane couldn't help her. "They killed her while we sat here, waiting. We did nothing. You told me you had people looking for her and yet, you didn't stop this, Shane. And now she's dead."

He gave her a pleading look. "We do have someone on this. You should have let me listen in. This could be a trick." He reached for Katherine again, remorse turning his blues eyes to a muted gray. "I'm sorry."

Katherine pushed at him, freeing her hands from his with a twisted tug. "You're sorry? That's all you can say? You just stood there and accused her of keeping tabs on me and being a part of this horror and she's dead. Dead. And you're sorry." Her hands at her side, she said, "You've failed again, Warwick. But this time, I'm the one who's lost someone I love."

Shane stepped out of his calm. And she was glad. Although she hated the hurt fusing through his eyes, she wanted him to feel the same gut-wrenching numbness that had her paralyzed.

"They might be lying to you," he said, his tone urgent, his gaze shattered. "They want to scare you out of hiding."

"They tried that, remember? They put Trudy on the phone even while they were abusing her. And you held me here anyway."

"I had no choice, Katherine. They sent people here to capture you. I had to stop them."

"Well, you did. You stopped them from harming me but Trudy didn't have a protector, did she?"

She whirled to leave, her only thought of getting away from him and the dormant longing and need he'd awakened in her. But her grief overpowered that need right now. Then she pivoted at the door. "I'm sorry, too. Sorry that I ever trusted you or listened to you." She pointed a finger in the air toward him, sobs choking her. "And I will never forgive you for this. Never."

Then she ran all the way upstairs to her room and slammed the door shut.

Shane held her watch in his hands, the warmth of her skin still lingering on the gold, the chill of her parting words still lingering on his heart. She hated him now, blamed him for this. And maybe she had a right to blame him.

Paco, who had a way of sinking into the shadows of a room, cleared his throat from behind a chair. "I tried every way to set up a trace, man. We ran out of time."

Shane put his hands on his hips. "She refused to let us listen in. But I'm sure she's been threatened again." He lifted the glistening watch. "I need you to take this apart. Look for anything that could be a GPS chip."

Paco stepped into the light and took the watch. "I'm on it."

Shane watched him leave then held onto his own chair. Had he been wrong all along? Was Trudy Pearson just an innocent bystander, collateral damage in a case that seemed to twist and change right before his eyes?

Wondering if he could have prevented this, he thought back on everything. No. He knew something wasn't right with Trudy. He'd watched her the night of the gala, making her rounds, working the crowd. It was his business to watch anyone who happened to be close to Katherine. And that night, Trudy had seemed too close, too observant, and too keen on Katherine's every move. At the time, Shane had chalked it up to their being such good friends and the fact that Trudy was helping Katherine with the festivities. But after reviewing all the information on Trudy Pearson, he'd ramped up the apprehension a notch on this woman. That apprehension had only increased when no one within the ranks of CHAIM had been able to locate Trudy.

What had he seen that night?

Thinking back, he remembered Katherine had ordered a sparkling water. They'd chatted, glancing his way. He remembered the way Katherine had only given him a passing glance while Trudy's gaze had stayed on him a long time.

Shane closed his eyes, reliving that moment in his mind, his stomach burning with an urgent fire. The waiter had handed Katherine her water and then he'd winked at Trudy. She'd leaned close to whisper something in his ear before she turned around to continue her conversation with Katherine.

The waiter!

Shane's pulse came back alive with such a quickening he had to inhale a breath. And then the whole picture came into his head, full-blown and crystal clear. The waiter. The same waiter who'd stood behind the stage with a gun aimed on Katherine. He'd changed his look, combed his hair differently and added a mustache but it was the same man.

Shane had to be sure. He quickly called Kissie, asking her to compare the surveillance video the hotel had downloaded to CHAIM. "See if you can get a match on the waiter who served Mrs. Atkins and her friend Trudy." He described Trudy and an estimation of the time. "Compare that image to the one we have of the shooter."

Kissie went to work on that while Shane tried to get his own visual on the events of that night.

He kept his eyes closed, going over each detail with a renewed emphasis. In his mind he could see the waiter with the gun hidden underneath a linen napkin, could see the man's intense gaze as he searched the room and spotted Katherine. Shane remembered pushing Katherine to the floor and shouting for everyone to get down. He'd watched the crowd, his gaze locking on the man who'd planned to quietly make the silenced shot then get away undetected. But after Shane had spotted him, the shooter had crouched down and moved with purposeful intent through the frightened, shocked crowd. Everyone had fallen down behind chairs and tables, hiding after the first shot had missed Katherine.

Except for one person.

Trudy Pearson hadn't ducked down at first. She'd just stood there behind the refreshment table, staring out into the crowd.

Until the caterer had tugged her down beside him.

Shane opened his eyes, the truth staring him in the face. He'd wondered time and again why they'd tried to kill Katherine that night but had gone to great lengths since then to keep her alive until they had her.

And now he knew the reason.

Trudy Pearson had been in on the hit that night. But now she was fighting to capture Katherine, not kill her.

Had she believed she'd be able to find something on Katherine that night, in that room?

The gunman had missed Katherine then turned toward Trudy Pearson for guidance and when he failed to do the job, someone else had come for both of them.

She'd called here, trying to get Katherine to help, maybe hoping to redeem herself somehow, too? Or to save herself by sacrificing Katherine? What did the two of them know?

Or rather, what did Trudy know?

Whatever it was, she could be dead now because of it.

He stared down at his desk, the papers blurring before his eyes as he remembered Katherine's parting words to him, remembered the venom in her gaze, the hurt in her voice.

She'd never forgive him for this.

And he'd never forgive himself. He had failed again.

Because of his actions, Katherine's best friend might now be dead. And whoever had killed her would surely come after Katherine with a renewed vengeance.

Then another image came into his mind. One of Katherine rushing out of this room with the cell still in her hand.

Shane looked out into the dark hallway then sprang into action. He had to get that cell phone away from Katherine before they called again. And this time, he'd do the listening.

SIXTEEN

Katherine slowly backed the little Miata out of the garage, turning off the automatic head lights until she could make it to the gate. Glancing in the rearview mirror, she was glad to see no one had noticed she'd left. Since she knew the garage code, she hoped the security system wouldn't even register she'd opened it. And she'd taken one of the remote controls to the main gate, too.

Not proud of having to stoop to theft to escape, she told herself she was doing this for the good of everyone involved. These people obviously wanted something from her and now she was going to give it to them, one way or another, and on her own terms. She had the phone on the seat in case they called again. And she had the revolver Paco had recovered from the road tucked safely in her bag.

So why were her palms so sweaty she could barely control the steering wheel?

Well, for starters, she was leaving Shane behind and his solid presence had made her feel safe over the last week or so. But Kit couldn't get past her anger or her grief. She wasn't ready to admit all the other feelings Shane brought out in her. And she might be going to a fate worse than she could imagine but she had to do this to stop the violence. She couldn't live like this anymore. These people were ruthless but she didn't have a choice. They wanted her and they were willing to kill others to get to her. She only prayed she could talk to them and hopefully help them find what they needed then somehow get away alive.

They'd killed Trudy.

They'd try to kill her, too.

And for what? Katherine didn't know anything. Didn't want to know anything. But her dead husband had obviously become mixed up in something criminal and now she was paying dearly for that. At least this way, she could find out the truth that so many people seemed to want to hide from her. And she'd start by going back to her office to do some research on the documentation they'd saved regarding her work in Mexico. That had to be the key. Either someone close to her had a criminal connection in Mexico and somehow thought Kit knew about it, or her husband had done something against the law and they needed to destroy the evidence and get rid of her, too.

She made it to the gate. Pushing buttons on the tiny remote, Kit waited for the big gates to slide back so she could get through. She'd have to find her way back to the main road without the help of the GPS system. Hopefully, she'd be well on her way before anyone alerted Shane.

Praying that Shane and the others back at the house wouldn't notice she was missing for a while, she shifted gears and hurried the eager little sports car along the curving lane. When she passed the spot where the road dipped into what was left of the mud hole, Kit couldn't stop the shivers coursing through her body.

No trace remained of what had happened here earlier. The big truck had been moved and all signs of the shootout had disappeared. Feeling as if she'd lived two lifetimes in the last few days, Kit carefully drove around the deep ruts and hurried out to the main road.

Shane had just left Paco busy working on the watch and was on his way to find Katherine when he heard the beep and knew instantly what had happened. He raced through the house, his gaze locking on the entry code by the back door. Usually the code read green if the house was secure. But right now it was reading red. And then it blinked green again.

He rushed out the door and watched as the garage light also went from red to green. Then he heard the doors to the other side sliding down.

Someone had left the premises in a vehicle.

Pulling out his phone, he called Paco. "We have a problem. I think the subject is on the run. In a yellow sports car."

"And you never saw that coming?"

Shane hated Paco's deadpan way of cutting to the chase. "I never thought she'd try this, no."

"Go after her. I've got everything else covered. Oh, and Warwick, I found a tiny GPS chip in the watch. The signal was weak but I disabled it anyway."

Shane's stomach muscles tightened in dread. "Try to jam the censors on the gate. Maybe we can stop her."

"I'm on it."

Shane hopped into his truck and peeled rubber as soon as the garage doors were clear. He prayed, asking

God to protect Katherine. Surely she wasn't going to meet these people on her own. That would be like writing her death sentence. Why would she do such a thing? Maybe to show him she didn't need his services anymore, since he'd failed her? Pushing that aside, he reasoned they'd probably threatened someone else close to her, using Trudy's murder as collateral.

His heart ripped at his rib cage at the thought. Katherine would do anything to stop this, to protect those around her. She'd lost Trudy so now she had some sort of death wish that could only lead to tragedy.

And Shane couldn't let that happen.

Not to the woman he loved.

Kit looked straight ahead, the muted lights dotting the city causing her eyes to glaze over. Exhaustion tugged at her, making her lids droop. She'd been on the road for over three hours and no one had tried to call on that infernal phone. And the man had said he'd call back in a couple of hours.

Her skin crawled with energy and her nerves twisted like tumbleweed. She wanted to cry for the death of her friend, but no tears would come. Maybe because Kit was burning with such a rage of fire, everything inside her burst into flames with each thought.

Soon she'd be in her office in downtown Austin. She'd pushed the little car to the limits and only refueled at the last possible minute, circling around and back to the gas station to make sure she wasn't being followed.

Remembering how Shane had driven the little car too fast to get her to safety at his ranch and done the same thing when he'd stopped for gas, Kit shook her head to block out that memory, her guilt at running away eating at her almost as much as her feelings for Shane.

Dear God, I know he's trying to help me but at what cost? What price for my salvation, Lord?

Her thoughts fluttered to the memory of his kiss. Had she ever been kissed that way before? Kit tried to remember Jacob's kisses but she had to block those bitter memories, too. The last time he'd kissed her was the night he'd given her the pearls and in her heart, she'd known his touch was full of betrayal.

Oh, Lord, help me. I feel so sick, so tired. Why did I ignore the truth? Why, Lord? Help me to understand.

The phone on the seat buzzed to life with a shrill jingling, causing Kit to gasp. Her hands shook as she gripped the steering wheel with one hand while she grabbed for the phone with the other one. She was a block from her office so she pulled off onto a side street.

"Hello?"

"Mrs. Atkins, so good to hear your voice."

"What do you want?"

"We want to talk to you. Ask you a few questions."

"I want to talk to you, too. So we can end this."

"Where are you?"

Katherine almost blurted it out but then decided to give them a taste of their own medicine by being cryptic. "I'm not on the ranch anymore. I'm close to Austin."

"And are you alone?"

"Yes."

"Very good."

"Where do you want to meet me?"

"There's an old warehouse on the river. Be there in one hour." He gave her the address. "And Mrs. Atkins, if Shane Warwick shows up, we'll kill him before we discuss anything with you, do you understand?"

"Yes. He won't be there."

The phone went silent in her hand. Leaning against the steering wheel, she took a breath then wiped at her eyes.

Kit was shaking so hard, she had trouble finding the entryway to the parking garage of her office. Very few cars were parked here this time of night—another warning for her to be careful. After what seemed like hours, she finally pulled into her assigned spot then changed her mind and parked one floor up, all the while watching for any cars moving toward her.

Stopping the little car, she took a deep breath, her hands gripping the steering wheel as if it were a lifeline. She glanced around to make sure she was alone then sat silent for a minute, leaning her head against the wheel, her prayers scattered and choppy as she asked God to protect her, to comfort her, and most of all, to keep Shane away from her for just a little while longer.

He was two car lengths behind her and gaining when she pulled over on the deserted downtown street.

Shane downshifted and stopped in the street as he watched the bright little butterfly of a car parking up ahead. Careful to stay out of her sight, he slipped the truck into a nearby open parking lot and shut off the headlights. He'd found her on the interstate and stayed with her, watching her gas up and admiring the tricks of the trade she'd obviously learned from her father and from watching Shane, no doubt. But being careful wouldn't stop these criminals from harming her. Only he could do that.

His phone rang, startling him. Praying it was Katherine, he answered it, his eyes on the car ahead. "Warwick."

"Brother, I've got some news," Paco said, his voice low and strained. "Kissie reported back—got a match on the waiter and the shooter. Same man. We've sent the information to the Austin police. And based on our suspicions about Trudy Pearson, we were able to get a definite on how and when she bought the phones. Got 'em the day after the gala shooting—from several different discount stores all over the city."

"Good," Shane said, gritting his teeth. "Maybe the Austin police can get the shooter to talk since the evidence is building. Make sure they know about the phones."

"Yep on the phones. And let's hope the shooter spills it. The lone survivor from this morning's shoot-out died at the county hospital about an hour ago. And I'm thinking it wasn't from his gunshot wound."

"Someone got to him?"

"Let's just say things looked suspicious, according to my sources."

Shane hit the steering wheel. "Any good news, Paco?"

"Yeah. But it won't make you smile. After talking to some of the subject's interns and aides, Kissie managed to dig up some pictures from one of the subject's trips to Mexico. And she found something very interesting."

"Oh, what's that?" Shane asked, making sure Katherine hadn't spotted him. He held his breath when he saw her slumped over the steering wheel.

"Seems Kissie found a picture of Senator Atkins with a woman in the lobby of a Mexico City hotel where some of the foundation's staff members were staying. And she wasn't his wife."

Shane kept his eyes on Katherine. She lifted her head and wiped at her eyes and his gut clinched. "We suspected as much," he said into the phone.

"Yeah, but we never expected the other woman to be Trudy Pearson."

"Trudy? You have proof that she's the woman in the picture?"

"Kissie's compared photos. It's her all right."

"She did go on a few of the mission trips with our subject. Maybe the subject was nearby?"

"Negative on that. Not in this particular shot. The intern who gave it to Kissie did so under duress after being interrogated by Mr. Barton himself. Was told by the senator to destroy the picture but said intern saved it, just in case."

"Are they in a compromising position?"

"No, but they look mighty cozy."

The tiny yellow car pulled back out onto the empty street. "Got to go. Good work, Paco."

"Later."

Shane waited until he saw Katherine turn the corner into the parking lot to her office building, then he parked the truck and started out on foot toward the building.

Telling herself security cameras were on her and she'd be safe because of that, Katherine rode the elevator to the fifth floor and breathed a sigh of relief when no one was waiting for her in the hallway. Hurrying to her office, she slid her key card into the slot and quickly locked the door behind her. Then she hurried to her files and began searching for any information she could find on her last trip to Mexico as well as the one planned for next month.

But everything regarding Mexico had disappeared.

She sat down at her desk, a single light on as she read through reams of paper and searched the computer files, too. Where were her files on Mexico? What if Jacob had some sort of secret files she didn't know about?

Maybe her donor list would give her a clue, since they had to keep accurate records on each donation. Hitting computer keys, she tried to pull up the list but couldn't find it. After several attempts, she knew the reason why.

The file had been deleted. It was gone.

And she couldn't find the hard copy in any of the folders on her desk or in the file cabinet.

Someone had swiped her donor file and all the information regarding the project in Mexico.

Kit got up to look around, hoping maybe the files had been moved for her protection or for the privacy of her clients. But that didn't make any sense either—unless her father had taken the files to help her out by protecting her patrons.

Finally, tired and frustrated, Kit glanced at the time on the computer screen. She'd have to hurry to make the meeting at the warehouse. And she still didn't have any more information than when she'd arrived, nothing to plead her case with these people who wanted to talk to her so badly. And no time to get to Jacob's files.

Sending up a prayer for guidance and protection, Kit turned off the lights and shut the door of her office.

When she turned around, a strong arm grabbed her from behind while a big hand went over her mouth.

Then a familiar voice rasped into her ear, "Don't move and don't make a sound."

SEVENTEEN

Katherine twisted in his arms, adrenaline and terror abating as she realized Shane was holding her. His hand gently held her arm and his clean country scent surrounded her. And yet, she wasn't ready to forgive and forget.

"Listen to me," he said, his mouth pressed to her ear. "We're not alone."

She gulped back the fear threatening to overtake her. Moving her head again, she tried to speak.

"I'm going to remove my hand but you can't say anything. We have to get out of here, now."

She nodded. He kissed her temple then lifted his hand away. "Just do as I say."

She should have done that all along. She should have listened to Shane and stayed with Shane. Now she'd brought him right into even more danger. Maybe she could get away from him if she acted angry. Then she pointed to her purse and mouthed "gun."

"Forget that for now."

He urged her forward toward the stairs, a finger to his lips. Slowly, carefully, he opened the door to the stairwell, his gun at the ready. When he saw that it was safe, he shielded her with his body as they made their way to the next floor. Glancing both ways, he finally turned to her and pulled her into his arms. "Don't ever leave me again."

Katherine fell against him then pulled back. "Let me go, Shane. You're no longer needed."

"I don't care," he said. "*I* need to be here."

His lips on hers cut off her attempt to sway him and took her breath and her anger away. It was enough for now that he was with her and she was back in his arms. It was enough, but her worries for him, coupled with the hurt of losing her friend, overruled her love for him. Later, when she knew he was safe she'd tell Shane the truth.

She loved him. And she'd do anything in her power to protect him. But beyond that, her mind blurred into a haze of pain. Because she could never have a life with the man who caused her best friend to die.

He loved her and he'd do anything in his power to protect her, Shane thought as he tiptoed with Kit down the stairwell. But she was still hurt and angry. He didn't think they'd ever get past that. But right now, he had to get her past the people who wanted to do her harm.

Just a few feet to the next exit and the parking garage but he wasn't certain of the big garage's security measures so he planned to take her out the same freight door he'd entered. They might have a chance once they'd made it out to the street.

"Who's following us?" she whispered when they stopped.

"Two men, dressed in black and carrying impressive weapons." Shane put a finger to her mouth. "We'll talk later."

His cell vibrated, then beeped the ASAP code. Paco with an urgent update. Guiding Kit to a dark hallway near the doors of the freight entrance, he pointed to the cell. "I need to check this."

It was a text:

"Urgent. K broke into encrypted files. T and J Petro-stolen oil from remote Mexican pipeline near village where subject mission work continues. TJ shell corporation owned by Pearson Industries. T and J is acronym—Trudy and Jacob. Selling stolen oil to unsuspecting U.S. refineries—with help from drug cartel—money missing. Someone found out—not happy. Careful, brother. 'Everything that is hidden or secret will eventually be brought to light and made plain to all.'"

Shane hissed a breath after reading the verse from Luke. This was big and deep and far-reaching and someone wanted to keep it secret and hidden. They'd never let Katherine live if they thought she knew about this. Siphoning off oil from a Mexican pipeline to ship into the United States and sell? Working with a drug cartel?

"Let's go," he told her as he tugged her through the freight doors.

"No. Not until you tell me what's going on."

The first bullet hit two inches from Shane's head. And the next one hit him in the left shoulder, knocking him to the ground.

Shane's left arm filled with a burning fire of pain. He struggled to stay conscious, Katherine's screams echoing inside his head.

* * *

Katherine bit at the rag they'd stuffed in her mouth, fibers of twisted material gagging her as the silent scream shouted inside her head. They'd blindfolded her so she had no way of knowing if Shane was alive or dead.

He hadn't answered when she'd called out his name right before they'd tackled her and put a gag on her mouth.

Please, God, let him be alive. Please, God.

That prayer kept her going, kept her from passing out or going hysterical. They were taking her somewhere in some sort of big truck. The gears shifted and groaned each time they stopped and started. Where was Shane?

She tried to twist her tied hands, hoping to free herself but a foot on her leg halted her. "Don't move."

Katherine sank back against what felt like packing blankets, praying that if she did as they asked, they'd spare Shane. Or was he already dead?

When the truck finally ground to a halt, she felt a strange sort of relief. At least now maybe she'd come face to face with her tormenters and get this over with, one way or another.

Shane groaned, a lit fuse of agony racing through his arm as he was lifted and dragged into a dark, damp room and dumped onto a pile of cold, dirty plastic. Looking through the slits of his closed eyes, he got around the haze of pain enough to see Katherine, tied up and gagged, being shoved onto a chair. She lifted her head, the dark blindfold unable to hide her fear or her anger. He prayed she'd think carefully about how to handle this. He prayed she wouldn't do anything rash.

He recognized the setup. Interrogation and torture.

His first instinct was to scream so loud they'd turn from her and put all their attention on him. But then, they'd probably finish him off and move back to her. He was expendable at this point. She was not—at least not until they'd tried every means possible to get information from her.

So he closed his eyes against that disturbing image, dropped his head and thanked God for the small blessing—and deadly mistake on the part of their tormentors—of not being gagged, tied and blindfolded as she had been. The only reason they'd brought him here was to make sure he died a slow death right in front of their eyes, or to make Katherine suffer as she watched him die. He didn't plan to oblige them, however. He wasn't going to die tonight. And neither was Katherine.

Katherine continued to take deep, calming breaths. Her father had taught her this when she was young and she'd had nightmares. "Just breathe, baby. Breathe and let God's love shield you from any monsters in your dreams." Her father would pat her hand then hold it tightly in his, the warmth of his strong grip making her feel safe and loved. "God will be with you, Kit, no matter what life throws at you."

Focusing on her daddy's words and his face as he'd tucked her back in and sat by her bed until she drifted off to sleep again, Kit asked God to shield her in his love and grace right now. And she asked the same for Shane.

She only prayed that wherever Shane was, he still had breath left in his body. Please, Shane. Stay alive.

Wishing she'd told him there on the stairwell that she loved him, Katherine pushed at the tears piercing her eyes. She listened to the movements around her. Chairs dragged across the concrete floor. Voices whispered in anger. Somewhere in the distance, she heard thunder rumbling. She thought she heard a woman's voice echoing across the air.

The fishy smell of the river assaulted her from an open window or door nearby. She could hear the slight flapping of some sort of curtains and feel the wind hitting her hot skin. They must have brought her to the warehouse they'd told her to meet them at—the deserted warehouse where no one would find her.

Get your bearings and get a plan, she told herself. Focus, Kit. Focus and listen. Find an opportunity, any opportunity.

Shane squinted, opening one eye enough to see that he was being loosely guarded by one man while the other stood staring down at Katherine. If he could make himself stay still and keep pretending to be unconscious, he might be able to save Kit. And if he could hit the right app on his phone screen, he could alert Paco to send help. He'd have to move very slowly but he thought he could find enough strength to take out the man guarding him. And maybe gain a weapon in the process.

Maybe.

Sweat moved in a slow, wet crawl down his spine and his arm throbbed and oozed blood, but he gritted his teeth against the pain and waited impatiently for someone to make a move. They were waiting on the big dog.

And it didn't take long for that person to show up. Shane heard the tap, tap of footsteps and surmised this was not a man. But then, this was no surprise to him. He had a feeling he knew exactly who'd just entered the dirty, dark warehouse.

"Take the blindfold and gag off her."

Kit gasped at the sound of that voice, her stare clashing into Trudy Pearson's the minute the blindfold was lifted away from her face. Shock kept her from speaking once the disgusting gag was gone, but a heated rage coursed through her body, giving her renewed determination. Shane had been right all along. And she might not ever get the chance to tell him how sorry she was for not believing him.

"Hello, Katherine." Trudy smiled sweetly, looking fresh and very much alive in her designer jeans and lightweight cream linen jacket, her chic black ankle boots tapping on the concrete floor. "What's wrong? You look like you've seen a ghost."

Katherine watched Trudy smiling over at the henchman holding a gun close to Katherine's temple—the head of catering from the hotel—and thought about spitting on her. Instead, she braced herself and decided she didn't need to use proper manners tonight but she wouldn't give Trudy any satisfaction by stooping to her level either. "I think I've had my fill of ghosts, Trudy. Yours and Jacob's. Why don't you tell me what's going on."

Trudy leaned down, giving Katherine a harsh glare.

"You're too stubborn for your own good, Kit. Why did you have to run off with Shane Warwick? It's so unseemly for someone as uptight as you, after all. Besides, we both know you can't keep a man happy."

Katherine ignored that jab and cut her gaze across the dark room, her heart leaping when she saw a still figure lying on a pile of plastic sheeting a few yards away. "Shane was protecting me. Doing his job."

Trudy glanced over to the man on the floor. "Yes and he did such a good job, I was beginning to think I'd never find you again. But here we all are, together at last. Your protector is either going to bleed to death or get himself shot again right in front of your eyes. I haven't decided which yet." She grinned. "Of course, if you tell me what I need to know, I might let him live for a little while. After you're gone, of course."

Katherine's stomach churned but she held her head up. She didn't want to give in to Trudy's demands, but she didn't have a choice. "What is it that you think I know? Is it worth all the trouble you've gone to or the lives you'd taken?"

"I think so," Trudy replied, her cold eyes burning with a heated intensity. She motioned to her caterer-kidnapper friend. "Pull me up a chair. This is a long story."

Shane listened, not daring to breathe, as Trudy Pearson promised to end the mystery and tell what had to be a fascinating if not twisted tale. He listened, his right hand inching toward his pocket, only to discover his cell phone was gone. No help there other than the alert he'd sent to the CHAIM satellite earlier when he'd been tracking Kit. Meantime, he'd have to do this the old-fashioned way, with sheer will and a determination to keep Katherine alive.

He prayed for a solid armor of Christ. He'd need every inch of the protection to get through this night. But for now, he could only wait for the right opportunity while he listened to Trudy's confession.

Fortunately, his guard seemed as interested as Shane. The man hadn't glanced his way since Trudy had entered the room and he was now sprawled across a chair, his gun relaxed at his side. And the man he now recognized as the catering manager who'd taken Trudy home the night of the gala was all ears, too. She must have promised them something big.

"I do owe you an explanation," Trudy said through a smirk. "This started before either of our husbands died. You know how these things go. I got bored when Gus was away on business."

Kit took in that bit of information with a shake of her head. "So you decided to amuse yourself with my husband?"

Trudy made a face. "It wasn't that hard, darling. You sure didn't give him much attention."

Kit leaned forward, straining against the ties. "I trusted you, Trudy. I told you all my fears regarding my marriage. I tried to give Jacob love and support. But it was never enough. Never."

"Apparently not," Trudy replied. "He liked my way better."

Shane's heart went out to Kit. She looked so small, so shocked that he almost got up and went to her. But then she lifted her head and he saw the serene look on her face and marveled at her calm in the face of this betrayal. But this calm could turn deadly at any minute and he had to be ready.

Kit couldn't believe she'd ever trusted this evil woman. How could she have been so gullible, so ignorant?

"So you had an affair with Jacob. How did that lead to this? You've killed people—" She stopped, a low moan choking her throat. "Did you kill Gus?"

Trudy's laugh sounded like brittle glass hitting against stone. "Goodness, no. Gus died of natural causes. I really did care about him but I was in love with Jacob. And he loved me. And we actually owe it all to you, Kit. It happened down in Mexico on one of your tedious mission trips."

Kit closed her eyes, the image of Jacob with her best friend turning her stomach. "No wonder you seemed so excited about going. And you obviously mixed business with pleasure down there. Where does the illegal activity come into play?"

"You always did know how to carry on with witty rapport," Trudy said through a tight smile. "Your husband managed to hook up with a drug cartel down there. You never knew he had a little addiction. He hid it pretty well, but the man was addicted to money and power. It was one of the things I loved about him." She waved a hand in the air. "Anyway, he cut a deal with a drug cartel to make some serious money."

"Drugs?" Kit asked. "Jacob was bringing illegal drugs into the country?"

Trudy shook her head. "Oh, no. He found something worth a lot more than drugs." She grinned then ran a hand through her hair. "Oil, Kit. All rerouted from a big pipeline to a secret pipeline manned by a cartel. We set up a dummy company and backed up the tankers and let it flow. We found a small independent company willing to look the other way and just like that, we were off and running. It was brilliant."

Kit tried to follow Trudy then decided her former friend was quite mad. "You can't be serious."

"Deadly serious," Trudy replied. "We had it all. He was going to leave you. But something went wrong with the cartel and, well, they said we shorted them of a few million. Jacob hid that money. Even from me, the scoundrel. Only, I really need that cash to save myself."

"I don't know what you're talking about," Katherine replied, her gaze sliding toward Shane's still body.

"No, you wouldn't. Too dumb to figure it out. But I watched you, tracked you and almost had you the night of the gala. I picked the hotel and I picked a few select workers to help me." She smiled over at the criminal caterer. "You were supposed to be shot, not killed. And I'd get to the money because I'd have access to you while you recovered. I figured out where the numbers to the safety deposit box were hidden, but I had to make it look like you were in danger."

She got up and with a vicious twist that seared Kit's neck, watched as Kit's glimmering pearls fell to the dirty floor. "The night he gave you these stupid pearls he was supposed to tell you about us. But he couldn't do it." Trudy handed one of the men the empty thread still attached to the heavy oval-shaped gold clasp. "Get the microscope and check the clasp. Look for numbers."

Kit fought at the tears streaming down her cheeks— tears caused by the raw torn skin on her neck and by the horrible truth of what had been going on right before her eyes. Jacob had given her those pearls for one reason. They held the key to all of this. "Did you kill my husband, Trudy?"

"How dare you!"

Trudy slapped her, the force of it snapping Kit's head back. When she straightened, she saw a movement in the shadows where Shane had been lying. He wasn't there anymore. She didn't dare let on that she knew.

She looked up at Trudy. "Tell me the truth."

"I did not kill Jacob!" Trudy shouted, her hand poised in the air. "I loved him. Those pearls were meant for *me*. And he wasn't supposed to get on that helicopter. You were!"

Kit gasped, realization breaking through the haze of horror surrounding her. "I'd scheduled an interview up in Dallas at the end of the week and Jacob had arranged to have a chopper fly me up there. But I never made the trip. Because he was killed that same week."

Trudy nodded, tears in her eyes. "Yes, there was a bad accident on the interstate that morning so Jacob took the chopper to the capital to avoid traffic. He didn't know I'd had it rigged to explode when you took your trip."

"Got the numbers, Trudy," the henchman-caterer said, coming back to give Trudy the gold clasp. She tossed it on the floor.

Grabbing Katherine's shirt, Trudy leaned in, her eyes wild with hatred. "I have what I want and I'm going to kill you and Shane Warwick. Then I'm going to give the cartel the money and I'm leaving the country. The cartel will let me live if I kill both of you. Do you understand now?"

Katherine understood everything now. Trudy's initial

plan had failed. But now, she had Katherine right where she wanted her. She'd probably made sure nothing could be traced back to her, including the tiny numbers engraved on the clasp of those broken pearls.

She'd sent those threats to Katherine as a smoke screen and she'd had someone search Katherine's house for the pearls. Then she tried to isolate Katherine. Hadn't Trudy suggested several times they go together to a remote spa? But Katherine had always been too busy. Thank goodness.

And then Shane had shown up.

"Is this why you want me dead?" she asked, aware that Shane was somewhere nearby. "You hate me because Jacob died in that chopper crash? Or because he still loved me?"

Trudy jerked a finger in her face. "You always had it all. The handsome, powerful man, the beautiful marriage and that blinding celebrity-status that drew people to you. It made me sick because it was all a facade. I had Jacob and the company we created together, until he got greedy. After he died, I tried to figure out a way to get those pearls off your skinny neck. It ends here."

Keeping her eyes on Katherine, Trudy raised a hand toward the man who'd been watching Shane. "Get Warwick and bring him here. I want you to kill him first."

Katherine saw a rising shadow off in the darkness. Shane. She had to protect him.

But it was too late. The guard turned to find an empty spot where Shane had been lying. "He's gone!"

Trudy whirled to stare into the darkness. "You idiot!" Grabbing the gun from the other man, she aimed and fired at the surprised guard, hitting him in the stomach.

And that's when Shane made his move, lunging for Trudy with a grunt. He knocked her down, rolled and grabbed the gun she'd dropped and took out the other guard before the man even had time to aim his weapon.

"Shane!"

"I'm all right," he said. Winded, he lifted Trudy to a sitting position then reached into her jacket pocket and found her cell phone. "Do you mind? I need to call 911." Shane did so, giving their location while he held the gun on Trudy. Then he called Paco Martinez and gave him the same information.

Trudy looked from Shane to Katherine, terror and madness in her eyes. "I can't let you live. You have to understand. I can't let either of you live. You know everything. They'll kill me."

Shane found some old rope and quickly tied Trudy's hands, holding her firm when she struggled. "You, my dear, talk too much. Too bad for you I have a very good memory."

Shane held the gun on Trudy with one hand while he reached around her and found the other weapon. "If you move, I'll shoot you," he told her as he walked backward toward Kit then went around her chair. Putting the gun on Kit's lap and keeping it aimed toward Trudy, he untied Kit then lifted her up. "How are you?"

"I've been better," she said. Then she reached up and hugged him close. "You're hurt though."

"I've been better," he mimicked, wrapping his working arm around her. "I'll be fine."

"Sit down," Katherine told him, pushing him down in the chair and taking his gun. Off in the distance, the urgent sound of sirens filled the night.

Shane didn't argue. But he smiled up at Katherine while she kept the rifle centered on Trudy Pearson. "Don't shoot her, luv. She wants to go away, remember? And now, she will, for a very long time."

"Kit?" Trudy looked genuinely scared now. "Kit, you can't let them arrest me. I'll tell them you were in on this, too. You wore those pearls day and night."

Kit walked toward Trudy, the gun centered on her, then bent down to pick up the gleaming gold clasp that lay by her feet. "I don't think that will wash, Trudy. Not when I give the money over to the authorities instead of your cartel."

"She's right," Shane said, his voice gravelly. "We've already found the encrypted files in your home and right about now, someone is probably doing the same at Kit's home, in the senator's study. We have all the evidence we need to put you away for a long time, Mrs. Pearson. We've also checked Katherine's files. They're clean."

"So that's where my files went," Katherine said, her gaze strong on Trudy.

"Sorry, luv. It was for your own protection."

For once, she was so very glad he'd said that.

Two weeks later

"Would you like more tea, dear?"

Katherine looked at Lady Samantha Warwick and shook her head. "No, thank you. Maybe I should go back to my hotel."

"Nonsense," the dark-haired woman said, her serene gray eyes reminding Katherine of her son. "Shane will be here soon. He's usually very prompt."

Katherine didn't respond. Shane was very prompt,

and very thorough and very...everything. So why was she in such a panic about seeing him again?

Because after he'd tidied up all the loose ends, he'd taken off for England with a whispered, "I'll be back, if you want me back."

Did he say that to all the women he saved?

"I'm so glad you came across the pond," Lady Samantha said, her gaze moving from the garden to the big stone and brick house on the hill. "Is this your first trip to England?"

"No." Kit admired the woman's manners. Filling time for her wayward son, no doubt. "But it's never looked more beautiful."

"Yes, we're having some good weather." Samantha sipped her tea then put down her cup. "Shane told me about what happened—without giving me the specifics. Horrible."

Kit nodded. "It was horrible."

Trudy had planned the whole scene at the gala, as a scare tactic to get Katherine to leave Austin. She'd hired several men eager to make some extra money and one of those men was supposed to "wound" Kit. Trudy intended to convince Kit to go to a secluded place to recuperate, so Trudy could steal the pearls that rarely left Katherine's neck. But she hadn't planned on Shane being at the gala. Shane, in the meantime, had figured out Trudy was behind everything.

While Kit had continued to defend her.

Was that why he'd left so abruptly? Did he think Kit still blamed him? He had been rather quiet their last day together at Eagle Rock, even when she'd tried to tell him she was sorry.

It didn't matter. Shane Warwick never stayed.

But he'd told her he'd come back one day, if she wanted that. She did. Very much.

So as soon as she'd given a statement and been cleared for travel, she'd come here like a silly school-girl, determined to declare her love for him, no matter the consequences. Because she was not going to let him run away from her love.

"He's changed," Lady Samantha said. "He's more centered and settled. In spite of what you went through, you've been a positive influence on my son."

Katherine decided to be honest about things. "Are you sure? He's known for not making a commitment, or so I've heard."

"Oh, yes, he's known for that but men have a way of changing once they fall in love."

"Is he in love with me?" Katherine asked.

Lady Samantha smiled then glanced over Katherine's shoulder. "Why don't you ask him yourself since he's standing on the terrace looking at you."

Katherine got up and whirled around, her gaze matching his. And without a word, she hurried toward him, her fast walk turning into a headlong run.

He met her in the middle of the garden, his arms opening in a welcoming embrace. "You're here."

Katherine smiled into the tweed of his jacket. "Only because you left me. I had to know why."

He pulled away to give her a relieved stare. "I was afraid."

"You? Afraid?" She could feel the wrapping on his bandaged left arm. "I don't believe that."

"You scare me," he said, crushing her back against him. "I wanted to give you time—"

"No, you wanted to give yourself time," she interrupted, tears in her eyes. "You had to see if this was real, didn't you?"

He looked sheepish. And adorable. "Okay, yes, maybe. But I fully intended to come and fetch you, one way or another."

"Fetch me? You intended to fetch me?"

"Or ask you to run away with me again."

She grinned up at him, her heart joyous. "Hmm. Let me see if I can get this straight. A dashing British secret agent in a precision-cut tweed jacket and a seemingly interested American woman in an overpriced sweater set. Their eyes meet across the country garden, they walk toward each other, smiling and cordial, and the rest is written in the stars."

"Oh, so you've seen that movie, have you?"

"Yes, and I know how it ends."

He reached out and touched a hand to her hair, pulling her toward him. "And tell me, luv, how does it end?"

"Happily ever after, of course."

"I like that ending." He kissed her right there in front of his mother, then lifted his head to gaze down at her. "I love you. I had to be sure though that you love me, so I left—to give you some time to work through your grief and the nightmare you went through."

"I do love you," she said. "I love you so much. And I tried to give *you* some space to work through your aversion to any sort of longtime commitment."

"So you came all this way to tell me that I'm afraid of commitment? And that you love me in spite of that?"

"Yes, I did."

"Did you meet my mother?"

"I did. Lovely woman."

"Do you want to get married in Texas or England, luv?"

Kit sighed and put her arms around him. "We could start here and work our way back to Texas for another ceremony. I'm sure Lonely Oak is lovely during the fall. And very safe."

He kissed her again. "It shall be doubly safe if you're there, darling. I'll make sure of that. But it won't be lonely anymore. We'll plant another oak—one we can show to our children." Then he took her by the hand and led her toward his mother.

Lady Samantha wiped at her eyes and smiled up at them.

While Katherine smiled up at the Knight who'd come to Texas to save her life. And capture her heart.

* * * * *

Dear Reader,

Have you ever wondered what it would be like to be swept off your feet by a handsome British secret agent? Okay, maybe not everyone thinks about spies the way I do, but it sure is fun to create a spy with a British accent. That's exactly what happened when Shane Warwick popped into my head. Shane, known as the Knight, was charming and cool—traits any good spy needs to have. I had to create a heroine who would match him in every way. Katherine Barton Atkins sure did that and more.

All fun aside, the seriousness of this story took hold of me, too. Katherine had been raised to always be a lady. Proper decorum and impeccable manners were a way of life for this Texas socialite. So it was very hard for her to grieve after her husband's mysterious death. And it was equally hard for her to accept Shane's protection and help. This theme seems a proper metaphor for how we sometimes push God away during times of pain and grief. It's hard to reach out and ask for help when we think we have to put on a good front all the time.

I hope this story entertained you and gave you an adventure and I hope the lessons Shane and Katherine learned showed you that God is always willing to help. It doesn't take a spy to tip us off on that. God is good all the time.

Until next time, may the angels watch over you. Always.

Lenora Worth

QUESTIONS FOR DISCUSSION

1. What traits in Shane Warwick showed he was a devoted Christian? How did his work contrast with his faith?

2. Why did Katherine fight Shane so much? Why was it so hard for her to see the betrayal in her life?

3. Katherine trusted her friends and family. Her loyalty was part of her whole upbringing. Do you think it's important to stay loyal to someone even if you don't trust them?

4. Shane had a dual citizenship in England and the U.S. Do you think this caused him conflict at times since his parents chose to live separate lives?

5. Katherine's family were devout and faith-centered. How did this help her through the trials of her life?

6. Do you think it was important to Katherine that Shane had a strong faith? How does this help a relationship?

7. Why did Katherine's best friend Trudy turn on her? Have you ever had a friend you trusted do something that is hard to forgive?

8. Katherine tried to help suffering people the world over by using her wealth and status to get things

done. Do you think wealthy people can be sincere in their need to serve God?

9. Why did Shane fight his attraction to Katherine? Do you believe he did the right thing by giving her some space after he left Texas?

10. Katherine found out her deceased husband had a lot of secrets. Have you ever found out things about someone you loved after that person died?

11. Do you think Katherine got past all the betrayal in her life? How will Shane help her to overcome the pain and love again?

12. Have you ever had a friend betray you in some way? How did you handle this?

Love Inspired®
SUSPENSE

TITLES AVAILABLE NEXT MONTH

Available September 14, 2010

LEGACY OF LIES
Jill Elizabeth Nelson

FORMULA FOR DANGER
Camy Tang

OUT ON A LIMB
Rachelle McCalla

HIGH-STAKES INHERITANCE
Susan Sleeman

LARGER-PRINT BOOKS!

GET 2 FREE
LARGER-PRINT NOVELS
PLUS 2 FREE
MYSTERY GIFTS

Love Inspired®

SUSPENSE
RIVETING INSPIRATIONAL ROMANCE

Larger-print novels are now available...

LISUSLP10R

Enjoy a sneak peek at fan favorite Molly O'Keefe's
Harlequin Superromance miniseries,
THE NOTORIOUS O'NEILLS, *with*
TYLER O'NEILL'S REDEMPTION,
available September 2010
only from Harlequin Superromance.

Police chief Juliette Tremblant recognized the shape of the man strolling down the street—in as calm and leisurely fashion as if it were the middle of the day rather than midnight. She slowed her car, convinced her eyes were playing tricks on her. It had been a long time since Tyler O'Neill had been seen in this town.

As she pulled to a stop at the curb, he turned toward her, and her heart about stopped.

"What the hell are you doing here, Tyler?"

"Well, if it isn't Juliette Tremblant." He made his way over to her, then leaned down so he could look her in the eye. He was close enough to touch.

Juliette was not, repeat, *not* going to touch Tyler O'Neill. Not with her fingers. Not with a ten-foot pole. There would be no touching. Which was too bad, since it was the only way she was ever going to convince herself the man standing in front of her—as rumpled and heart-stoppingly handsome now as he'd been at sixteen—was real.

And not a figment of all her furious revenge dreams.

"What are you doing back in Bonne Terre?" she asked.

"The manor is sitting empty," Tyler said and shrugged, as though his arriving out of the blue after ten years was casual. "Seems like someone should be watching over the family home."

"You?" She laughed at the very notion of him being here for any unselfish reason. "Please."

He stared at her for a second, then smiled. Her heart fluttered against her chest—a small mechanical bird powered by that smile.

"You're right." But that cryptic comment was all he offered.

Juliette bit her lip against the other questions.

Why did you go?

Why didn't you write? Call?

What did I do?

But what would be the point? Ten years of silence were all the answer she really needed.

She had sworn off feeling anything for this man long ago. Yet one look at him and all the old hurt and rage resurfaced as though they'd been waiting for the chance. That made her mad.

She put the car in gear, determined not to waste another minute thinking about Tyler O'Neill. "Have a good night, Tyler," she said, liking all the cool "go screw yourself" she managed to fit into those words.

It seems Juliette has an old score to settle with Tyler.
Pick up TYLER O'NEILL'S REDEMPTION
to see how he makes it up to her.
Available September 2010,
only from Harlequin Superromance.